THE SECRET HISTORY OF
ENGLAND

THE SECRET HISTORY OF
ENGLAND

JACK JUNIUS

authorHOUSE®

AuthorHouse™
1663 Liberty Drive
Bloomington, IN 47403
www.authorhouse.com
Phone: 1-800-839-8640

First published by AuthorHouse   01/28/2012

ISBN: 978-1-4678-8431-0 (sc)
ISBN: 978-1-4678-8432-7 (ebk)

Printed in the United States of America

Any people depicted in stock imagery provided by Thinkstock are models, and such images are being used for illustrative purposes only.
Certain stock imagery © Thinkstock.

This book is printed on acid-free paper.

CONTENTS

CHAPTER 1

THE LAST OF THE ROMANS

Helen was here again. The strange reddish stone of the walls and steps. Very frightening, and someone hurrying her, as she stumbled under the weight of the unseen objects she was carrying. The night air was cold, as she moved further up the broad flight of steps that led from somewhere underground. A voice behind her said "We're the last of the Romans." She was coming out onto open ground now. There were people standing crowded together in the darkness. She looked to her right, and saw fire in the distance, lower down in the valley —.

She woke, relieved to find it was a dream, but still frightened. The night-light on the chest-of-draws failed to give her comfort. She scrambled out of bed and into the corridor. A faint light at the end illuminated whitened walls. Still fearful, she hastened down the corridor, until a door opened letting out a blaze of electric light.

'Helen?' Her mother came out to her.

'I've had that nasty dream again.'

Her mother took her by the shoulder, and said,

'There's nothing to be frightened of. I'll come and read to you.'

They went back to her room. Her mother read her a favourite story about Queen Ygraine. It took quite a long time, but eventually she was asleep, and knew nothing until the morning. Then, however, the unpleasant memory of fear

1

lingered, and with it, the expectation that that dream would return.

*   *   *

Eighteen Years Later: — The Cotswolds: A.D. 2069

Everything was ready for tomorrow. The site office and all their equipment for the excavation to one side of the entrance, and on the other, his new motor home, giving him independence from the vagaries of rural accommodation. A slight haze of rain hung over steep banks of woods rising above a few fields that sloped down to a stream. A large modern house, a concoction of turf and solar panels, stood further up, close to the top of the little valley, where the lane narrowed down into a bridle track. In the opposite direction, lower down the valley, he could make out the church and other buildings in Northcombe village.

James saw a girl come in through the open field gate, and make for the site office. Tall, leggy, probably early/mid twenties. He needed some things from the office, so that would be an excuse to call in, and find out what was going on here. Stepping into the cabin, he heard Tessa, his site assistant, saying,

'No, I'm sorry, we don't have any vacancies for volunteers. A lot of young people want this type of work.'

The girl was turning to go. Close up, she was definitely a must have for any decent archaeological site, although there was something about the eyes, something you'd call wild, of frightened or perhaps the word was fey.

'Oh, just a moment,' he said, 'I think one or two of our people look like dropping out.'

Tessa frowned and said,

2

'You should have let me know,' and then to the girl, 'Are you studying archaeology, or have you worked on sites before.'

'No.'

'I don't think that matters,' he said quickly. 'We can use a novice, so long as you're ready for manual work.'

Tessa fiddled with some things on her desk, rather noisily, and then muttered,

'Give me your name, I'd better put you on the list.'

'It's, Helen Roberts.'

'We can't give you any travel expenses, we're over budget even with drop outs,' Tessa said.

'That's okay,' Helen replied, 'I live just next door. I'm your neighbour here.'

* * *

By the second week, the site had started to reveal itself. The first layer of earth taken up, and the foundations of masonry walls beginning to emerge. There was no doubt that Helen was the girl that he kept noticing, and who was starting to obtrude into his thoughts.

One evening, they went for a drink at the Eagle in Northcombe. He'd been taken aback by just how attractive she was, now dressed for the evening. This left him a bit flustered, and unable to think of much to say. The Eagle was all seventeenth century beams jostling promiscuously with fibre glass replicas and unfortunate brickwork from the previous century. There was an ambience of slightly grubby disorganisation, but prices that would have made a West End restauranteur blush. The suggested drink morphed into dinner.

'What made you choose us for your excavation?' Helen asked.

3

'There're indications of post-Roman occupation. That's a period I'm interested in. And it's a big site; never been touched, except a small amateur dig in Victorian times.'

'A lot of stuff had come to the surface, from when there was a farm up there,' Helen remarked. 'Coins and bits of pottery. We had them in the house. I used to play with them when I was young. Then somebody said they might be of interest, and we gave them to the museum.'

'They were right. They were one of the things that made me notice the site. You see I'm trying to fit this area, this villa particularly, into the larger picture.'

'Larger picture?'

'Yes,' he paused, wondering how to proceed. 'Well, it really goes back to some other digs, not just mine, from the last few years. What's been found—well, people disagree about the interpretation. Hm.—how can I explain it? Burials, they're important to us archaeologists, of course—they seem to indicate the presence of soldiers from the continent,—mercenaries probably. And related to that there've been some finds of Frankish gold coins related to the sites used by Saxon leaders.'

'Gold coins?'

'Payments for military actions, possibly. The Franks were the regional power then. Just across the channel of course.'

'I like that. Your personal theory. Not just copying out what big supervisor says.' Helen said.

'You sound like Branwen—my ex—she thought it ridiculous.—That's what finished us off.'

'You split up over a thing like that?' She sounded incredulous.

'No. We had other problems. But we managed to stick with it, while we still respected one another's ideas. Eight years. I met her when I went to work at the university. She's a historian. When she started pouring scorn on my idea, it didn't seem worth the effort any longer.'

'I see,' she muttered, scowling to herself. 'Well, it beats being used and dumped, I suppose.'

'You mean yourself?'

'We were both doing an MA in journalism,' she said. 'I'm trying to become a journalist. Not very successfully. That's why I'm living with my parents at the moment. Looking for something. Anyway, we were together for most of the MA time and for nearly a year afterwards. Then, well, he just decided to go to Africa indefinitely. Come out and see me, he said, but that would never work.'

'I'm sorry.'

He was silent for a moment, feeling suddenly embarrassed. He wondered, if she was thinking the same thing as he was. Nothing stood between them and something physical. That was ridiculous. This was just a drink, well, a meal, to while away a boring evening, stuck in the middle of nowhere.

'Go on, tell me more about your theory on the Franks? What do you think they were trying to do?' she said.

'Well, I've often used to feel there was something that didn't quite add up about the Saxon conquest of England. We're supposed to believe in a smooth, inevitable advance across the country. But they were checked at an early stage, and the more you look at it, the more it seems their rule was confined to quite small areas. Then a hundred years later they suddenly started winning battle after battle.'

'Sounds suspicious.'

'What's really suspicious, or at least a hell of a coincidence is that this comes at about the same time as the first missions to the Saxons from Rome. The regional power, the Franks had converted, and we know there were tensions between Rome and a possibly heretical British church. The Franks had already been very anti another heresy in Spain.'

'A crusade? Because of a spat with the British church,' Helen said.

'It seems mad to you, but heresy was hot then. It's quite feasible that something heretical in this country simply had to go. We know something like this happened much later on in the south of France.'

'I see.'

'I'm hoping that sites like this might give a clue to what went on. But could we just keep this crusade thing between ourselves. Not everybody's very happy about the idea. Officially, for the funding agency and so on, it's just a big Romano-British site. Don't mention anything to Tessa in particular.'

She was silent. Eventually, he said,

'Have you always been interested in history and archaeology?'

She shook her head.

'So, you were just curious about our excavation?' He continued.

Now, very strongly, he saw the look he had seen in her eyes when they first met, what he thought of as the fey look. She looked away, and started to play with a silver band, sliding it up and down her arm. He became slightly mesmerised by the handsome band and the even more attractive arm. When she showed no signs of stopping, he said.

'Sorry, I don't mean to pry or anything. You're very welcome to work on the site with us, of course.'

She looked up. He felt she was assessing him, as to whether she could trust him. Finally, she said,

'Your crusade is some sort of secret, well, this is much more of a secret.'

Then she told him about the dream of the steps and the Romans and the fire.

'It started when I was small,' she continued, 'when it didn't go away, they started talking about me seeing someone. I didn't want that, so I pretended I'd stopped having the dream. Later on, if they mentioned it, I made out I couldn't even remember what they were talking about. But it hadn't gone away, and I've had it more and more the last few months. It always frightens me. I often don't sleep that well. Sometimes, I'm too frightened to go to sleep, in case I have the dream.'

He frowned. Why did there always have to be something wrong with the girls he met. Here she was attractive, bright, agreeable. But now came something weird. Something that every archaeologist hated. People with dreams, visions and bizarre theories about their site.

'You say it's a wide flight of stone steps leading up from underground?' he said.

'Yes, that's how it seems.'

'Look, our site's probably going to turn out to be a villa. They never had large underground spaces. If there was anything underground, it would be more likely to be to do with the monastery. You know there was a small one here in the Middle Ages. Or even a blocked off cellar under your own house, from when it was a farm.'

'But the Romans —'

He was grateful now that he had always lived and worked in modern houses, flats, schools and universities. Living in this sort of place could perhaps start to work on your mind.

'It may have been something that just came from playing with those coins and bits of pottery,' he said. 'They may somehow have fired up your imagination. Anyway, when we've dug the whole thing up, and you can see it's just an innocent villa — two storeys and nothing underground, you'll see it's all nonsense, and you'll be more relaxed. That's one thing this excavation could achieve, if nothing else.'

She looked unconvinced, but they did not discuss it further. Their meal finished, they paid, left, and walked silently up the lane. He felt guilty. He didn't like holding something back, but telling her would only feed this thing. It was true the site hadn't been excavated in modern times, but his predecessor, a specialist in agricultural settlements, had excavated a post-Roman site on the edge of the village here. There he had found the clear signature of destruction by fire and a violent end to the settlement.

They paused at the entrance to the site. He thought of the empty darkness of the motor home. At times like this, he missed Branwen.

'Come in and have a coffee,' he said.

Damn. He hadn't meant to say that. He hardly knew her, and she might think he was after the quick shag. After eight years, he had got out of the etiquette of this sort of thing.

'Yes, I could do with a coffee,' she replied.

Inside, she admired the stylish arrangements, and then said,

'Actually, I'd prefer wine, if you've have anything.'

He got some wine. She drank, and then turned towards him with such a happy and open expression that without thinking, he lent forward and kissed her on the lips. He drew back quickly. That had blown it. She would see him as a crass lunger. She'd laugh about it with the other girls on the site, and he'd be an object of snide ridicule.

He needn't have worried, however, as she was already casting off her clothes.

Chapter 2

The Secret Church

Fire, fire and blackened beams that was all she could see. There was running, feelings of fear and panic and confused voices. Something about Honoria and the white town. The same sensations repeated over and over again. She knew this was somehow to do with that other time, when she came up the reddish stone steps, and saw the waiting group of people in the darkness. Then there was something solid under her, and her just-waking mind realised that this had not been real, and that she was safe in her bed at home. She reached over and put the light on, reassured now by the solidity of the familiar bedroom, the curtains across the large window, the treasured painting on the wall, the bedside table.

To her groggy mind, this dream was another unwelcome night—intrusion, coming on top of the recurrent dreams of recent months. She knew she wasn't going to go to sleep any time soon, so she got out of bed, slipped on her kimono, and went downstairs. As she did this, she remembered what had happened the previous evening. She'd had sex with James. That hadn't been meant to, or expected to happen. A drink with someone she worked with. Well, she supposed he was quite attractive, but he hadn't shown much sign of being interested, until he suggested that drink. Even then, she had seen it mainly as a chance to satisfy her curiosity about the history of the site. Had it been a mistake? Since the sixth form, she had embraced the recent fashion for repelling the fuck-and-forget brigade. They should be made to make at least a token show of more lasting interest. Now she had gone completely over board at the first sign of interest. Nothing more might have happened, if she hadn't more-or-less forced him. Maybe, subconsciously, she had been a bit competitive. She had caught him admiring Lizzie one day, when she had been bending over in a trench. Lizzie could have been next in line for the motor home experience, if she hadn't made a move herself. But the fact was, she realised as sleep began to clear from her mind, that what had happened felt completely right. She had a strange resonance with this archaeologist that she had hardly known until the previous evening.

She went into her work room. If she couldn't sleep, she might as well do something useful. A screen and a solitary desk lamp provided her only light. She drew back the curtains to reveal the darkness of the garden. It was June, which meant it would be getting light soon. James had mentioned an earlier Victorian dig at the villa. It struck her as strange that she had never thought to look up anything about the villa before. To her it had simply been a fact that there was something Roman and that her dreams were somehow connected to it. Well, now she could use this sleepless pre-dawn time to catch up on anything that was there.

It took some time, but eventually she closed in on what she needed. There was a brief summary of the Victorian excavation, which told her less than she already knew. But then she noticed something she hadn't expected. The write-up of an excavation from only five years before. Annoyingly, it required a payment to read the full text in a learned archaeological journal. She pondered whether it was worth it. She was short of money already, but in the end she registered the payment and brought up the article. It was written in an opaque style, and she decided to make some coffee, to get her early-hours mind through the material. By the time she returned from the kitchen, the birds had started their noise in the garden, the so-called dawn chorus, that brutal, raucous noise that warns insomniacs that their chance of a good night's sleep has slipped away.

She started reading seriously. The paper did not refer to the actual villa site, but to another probably related settlement centred on the large field just behind the village church. Now she vaguely remembered. She had been away on her gap year. The only thing that had really reached her was something about the villagers complaining, because of cars parked on the track behind the church.

Strange that James hadn't mentioned this excavation, particularly as it seemed to have been done by someone at his own university. The material was difficult and tedious to unravel. The sky had started to lighten to a cold dark blue, while the birds continued their racket. Then suddenly she had it, clearer sentences in the concluding paragraphs of the paper, 'destruction by fire', then, 'likely interpretation is a violent end to the occupation of the site', and finally, 'may feasibly be related to the end of the post-Roman occupation of the neighbouring villa site'.

First, she realised with a chill that a fire in the field behind the church would be clearly visible from the villa that she associated with most of her dreams. Next, with a flash of anger, she understood that James had been holding back on her. She had told him about seeing fire in the distance in her dreams. He must have known about the findings of the earlier excavation, but instead of mentioning the similarity to her dream, he had tried to fob her off.

She got up from the table. The garden was suffused with grey light; darkness clung around the hedges and trees. In the corner of her eye, something moved outside on the terrace—was it a fox? She turned to look, and just for a moment, she thought she saw flat spinning discs of fire, and then there was nothing there except dark paving stones gleaming wet in the morning air and the grass beyond. She must have imagined it she thought, but at the same time, a clear voice in her head said 'spirits of the dead'.

* * *

'So now you can start excavating my steps,' Helen said.

'Now, please—' James said. It was just his luck that his biggest break through, the discovery of a church inside the villa, had been the start of his difficulties with Helen. It had begun with that one reddish block of stone emerging innocently from under the trowels of the volunteers. Helen had said it was the colour of the stonework in her dreams, and that he should excavate there.

'I still can't see your problem,' she said

'Oh Helen, we've discussed this a hundred times. We don't do archaeology like that. This isn't Edwardian times. I can't dig up something because of a ghost or a dream. I have to account for public money.'

She frowned and said, 'Make up a reason.'

'I won't find any steps. I know how villas were planned. There are no steps there.'

'You're being a bit economical with the truth,' she said

'No.—What do you mean?'

'Two things. First, you didn't tell me about the fire in the village.'

'What?'

'The bloke before you at the university. He dug up a site. The same period as this. It'd been burnt. I've looked it up. You didn't tell me, yet you know I see a fire in my dreams.'

'Er—'

It was evening, and they were standing alone in the middle of the site. She went over to the reddish block of stone, pointed and said, 'His site was in that field behind the church. From here you'd see it, if there was a fire down there.'

He looked down the hill at the greens and greys of the summer view. She was starting to make him imagine the landscape as haunted. There was madness in this. What a pity. This thing spoilt her. She might seem more reasonable than Branwen, but at bottom, she was even madder.

'And also, I know you're lying about how villas were built.'

'No,' he replied, 'there're you're wrong'

'No, there's that place in the North Downs, Lullingstone. There's a cult room, or whatever they call it, right below the church.'

'All right, yes, but that's just one site.'

'There are only three other sites like this in the country anyway,' she retorted.

'We're over budget. I've got to concentrate on the bath house. I literally haven't even a day's worth of work to spare on anything else.'

'Your bath house!' Always the bloody bathhouse!'

'We've discussed why it's important. I really don't have a choice.'

'Your trouble is, you just lack guts. You had an idea that might just be interesting, but instead you're going to dig up the bathroom. I was mistaken about you. You're just a frightened little man. A frightened little bureaucrat, ticking boxes, rather than doing anything important. I'm getting out! I'm not coming to this site again, and I don't want to see any more of you.'

'The trouble with you is that you're just a spoilt brat. The moment you don't get your way, you throw a tantrum.'

'Fuck you!' she shouted, turned away from him, and hurried down the hill.

Oh, God, why did nothing ever run smoothly with girls. For a moment he had really thought they had something going. He made his way slowly back to the motor home. Inside, first thing, he reached for a bottle of red wine and poured a glass. Then he opened his computer, and had another look at the survey of the site. He scrolled to-and-fro through the document for a while, and then, suddenly, it seemed so boring. It was true, he'd rather dig under the church. He reached for his glass, found it nearly empty, and poured some more. He scrolled back to the part of the survey that covered the site of the church, and peered at it. Where her red stone was, there was in fact a small disturbance in the ground that could be indicative of perhaps a minor structure, or even a structure whose imprint faded as it went deeper into the ground. He replenished his again empty glass. Bottle three-quarters gone. Well, there were more in the rack.

The clarity of his mind was blurring a bit, but at the same time, he was feeling more powerful. No longer somebody who could be pushed around by spending constraints or research targets. He had an important theory, and he would follow it up. He still realised he had to justify anything he did at the site. But, perhaps she was right. Lullingstone was a precedent for an important underground space, and there was the slight disturbance of the ground, clearly indicated in the survey. They could just do some exploratory work, which would show there was nothing there. There were one or two short cuts he could make with the bath house to claw back the time.

He sent a message to Helen.

'You're right—will excavate by the red stone.—Hope to see you on site tomorrow.'

Her message came back,

'Glad you have come to your senses. Better than tomorrow, I'll come down there now.'

Chapter 3

Hotel in Harlech

Tessa came in with a determined step. James and Helen looked up from their lunch.

'What're you up to now,' Tessa said. 'We were supposed to be starting on the bath house this morning. Now, I'm told you're working right next to the church.'

'Oh, er, yes, sorry about that,' James muttered.

'Typical, you know I have to keep admin. posted every morning. How can I do that if you keep going off plan?'

'No, sorry. I was working late to do with the change of plan. I'm sorry, I simply forgot to mention it this morning. Could you just send an amendment to your last posting. Sorry, I know that's a bit of a bore.'

'It's not just that. I need to give a reason for the change. We're already behind schedule. They have been on at me about it several times. — Helen would you excuse us. I feel this is a private conversation.'

'Private?' Helen said.

'Yes, private,' Tessa replied.

Helen appeared to be shifting off her seat, as if to go, but then seemed to think better of it, and said, 'I've lived virtually on top of this site all my life. I feel I have the right to know what goes on here. I don't think your conversation can be that private.'

'Well really . . . James can you . . . no, you can't of course . . . I suppose, we could go to the site office?'

James glanced across the lunch table at Helen, and caught her gaze, which said as clear as could be, 'Back down on this excavation, and you're dumped, — lad.'

'It's not that private,' James said.

'You just give in, don't you? All right, if we must,' Tessa said. 'Look, you always get behind schedule. You asked me to stop it happening again, before we started digging here. But you've got behind just the same, and this new change is going to make it worse.'

'I know,' James said, 'but last night I made an assessment that we may have a major unanticipated feature on the site.'

'I think I'm going to have to call Professor Archibald. He ought to know about this.' Tessa turned and bustled out of the van.

They were silent for a moment, and James tried to resume his lunch, but then said,

'I think she might be a bit jealous.'

'Jealous?'

'Hm, I suppose the skeleton's got to come out of the cupboard sooner or later. A long time ago — ten years — we had a thing, — well just a one night stand.'

'You couldn't have done. I mean she's old.' Helen said.

'She's not that old. Only a few years older than me — well, I suppose she's eight years older.'

'Ah, of course, she's well endowed, as you'd probably put it. That's what you like about her.'

'Actually, I prefer a more discrete figure like yours.'

'Nicely put. I'll believe you, others wouldn't.'

'Ten years ago, she was only in her early thirties. I'm afraid she's rather let herself go since then. — Our thing was an accident. We were doing an excavation in north Wales. The loneliest fort in the Roman Empire, it was claimed. We were put up in this rather bleak hotel in Harlech. There was nothing to do. One night we got pissed in the bar, and ended up in her room.'

'It sounds like the sort of thing we were warned about in our sex education classes,' Helen said.

'It's my only one night stand. I was eight years with Branwen without . . .'

'Without looking at another woman.'

'Well, without touching another woman.'

'Clearly, you're a credit to your sex.' Helen said.

'You're not so slow yourself', James said. 'It was you who seduced me, and on a first date.'

'Ah, but I found you attractive, and I wasn't pissed either,' Helen said.

Attractive. She found him attractive. He'd never thought of himself like that. He'd always looked to a hard graft of trying to be persistently charming, and hoping there were some common interests. Sometimes a bit like the boy scout thing of rubbing two bits of cold, sodden wood together, and hoping to start a fire.

'Does Tessa know enough to judge what should be excavated?' Helen interrupted his thoughts.

'That's another thing where jealousy comes in,' James said. 'That time in Harlech, she was already the site assistant, and I was just a graduate student doing the sort of thing we've got you doing. Now I'm the site director, but she's still an assistant. She's spent the best part of the last ten years trying to get through an Electronic University degree in Practical Archaeology. That would allow her to run a small excavation, with a bit of long-range supervision.'

'Perhaps, you could have helped her. Maybe she's pissed off, because she thinks you owe her after Harlech.'

'I have helped her. Lots. The trouble is she panics with the essay questions, and tends to write nonsense. I've tried and tried to help with essay plans and strategies and all that sort of thing, but she just can't get a handle on it.'

'Can she stop you excavating where you want?' Helen asked. 'I thought the director of the excavation decided.'

'Yes, I decide, but she can make it difficult, if she get's Archibald on her side. I have the ultimate say, here and now, but going against him wouldn't be a great career move.'

'You bring it on yourself,' Helen said.

'I don't see . . . ?'

'You're too timid, too accommodating, afraid of confrontation. She wouldn't have tried it on like that, if you were more of a man.'

'I'm not sure.' James muttered.

'I am. It's the same in bed. You're so passive. You're like a teddy bear. I don't want to do it with my teddy bear.'

'I didn't get the impression you had a problem. Last night . . .'

'Oh, you're better than my last boy friend. You've got the right idea, but it's the way you go about it. You do have some good qualities. Kind, gentle, supportive, I suppose. But I need someone more assertive, dominant . . .'

There was the sound of heavy feet on the steps, and Tessa had returned. James had rather the impression that she might have caught the last part of their conversation.

'Professor Archibald would like you to give him a call,' Tessa said.

James reached for his phone.

'Oh, I think he'd like you to use the holophone,' Tessa said. 'Remember it's policy to use them. They aid staff communication with face-to-face contact.'

'I find it difficult to get a decent signal here. It's all these hills.'

'Really? I never have any trouble,' Tessa said.

'Your phone may be a later model,' James said

'Better give it a try, all the same.' Tessa said as she made her way out.

The holophone was a complicated device, already evilly crouching on the corner of the table. James moved the lunch things out of the way, and dragged the device towards him. It took a couple of minutes to jump through the various hoops that the system demanded.

'Very clunky,' Helen remarked. 'That's a Critterbridge 2066. They're crap. My father's firm all use Hanki Huukus. Better image and cheaper as well.'

At last, a shimmering image of Archibald appeared in a corner of the dining area. James could see his mouth moving but there was no sound. He searched through the controls, trying to remember how to adjust the sound. Helen was sitting opposite James, and in a position that would make her invisible to Archibald. She reached over to fiddle with some buttons hidden at the back of the machine, and then they could hear the professor's voice.

'I'm hearing you now,' James said.

'Good, never known anyone have any problems with these before,' Archibald said. 'Now this plan change. Of course, it has to be your decision, but you should consider it in the light of policy. 'Now . . .'. A surge of static blotted out Archibald's voice, and coloured squares marched across parts of his image. Helen reached over again, and started playing with a further set of concealed buttons.

'You must learn how to use your equipment properly,' Helen said. 'What if you had to do it on your own. I can't always be here.'

'It tends to blow up on me, if I touch anything unusual.'

'Why don't you ask Tessa. She might come in useful for once.'

'I don't think she knows how it works either. I'm sure she was bluffing just now.'

'It must be something to do with being archaeologists,' Helen said. 'You'd probably rather communicate by ear trumpet.'

After a time, Archibald's voice returned, but much of his speech was reduced to a mere burble, and it was interrupted by spikes of static. James strained his ears to make out what

Archibald was saying, '. . . policy . . . burble . . . crackle . . . funding . . . crackle . . . burble . . . government . . . burble, . . . crackle, . . . national policy guidelines . . . burble . . . crackle . . . Vice Chancellor said to me only the other day . . . burble, burble . . . crackle . . . fringe or pseudoscience . . . crackle . . . religious sites . . . crackle, . . . Fisher King . . . crackle . . . dark tide of the occult . . . crackle, crackle, crackle . . .'

'I'm sorry,' James interrupted, 'I'm not getting a lot of what you're saying. Could we do it on an ordinary phone.'

'Clear as a bell here. I haven't got any problem . . . crackle, crackle . . . burble . . . grail's always in the west . . . crackle, crackle . . . esoteric . . . crackle, . . . concealed . . . crackle . . . charitable donors . . . crackle, . . . alumni . . . crackle, . . . legacies . . . crackle . . . don't like that sort of mystic thing . . . burble . . . we should follow Hurstey, where he says the bath house is . . . crackle . . . to understanding Roman . . . burble, crackle . . . Byzantine trade routes . . . crackle . . . crucial . . . burble, burble . . . crackle, crackle, crackle.'

The coloured squares marched across the image again. Clunk. Image gone—nothing.

'Fuck!'

'Just try and get him on audio alone,' Helen said.

She fiddled with some of the concealed buttons. The thin but less than audible sound of a human voice emerged from the depths of the machine. Helen reached into a hidden compartment in the side of the machine, and produced and plugged in some head phones. James took these and put them on. Now at last he could hear Archibald's voice properly.

'I can't see you any longer. Are you having some sort of problem?' Archibald asked.

'We'll have to just do it on audio,' James said.

'Most unusual. I've never heard of anyone else having problems with these phones. A very good product, in my opinion. Must be something you pressed. There was nothing wrong with mine.'

There was a click. Helen had inserted another set of head phones, and was starting to listen in.

'Is there someone on the line? This could be confidential,' Archibald said.

James signalled to Helen to disconnect. She signalled back more emphatically that she wasn't going to. It was clear she was not going to take any notice of him. That was too bad. How could she carry on like that making a difficult situation more difficult. So thoughtless. So inconsiderate. Spoilt brat.

'No, no one's on the line, I was just making an adjustment,' James said.

'Well, there isn't that much more to say. You've heard the policy background.'

'Well, I didn't get everything. There was a problem with the sound.'

'Yes, yes. But you'll have got the gist. I can't stay with you much longer, my PA's trying to get me to go into a meeting. It's a priority. A bit of a crisis really. The quarterly meeting of the travel expenses senior committee. I think I've made clear the risks of your site strategy. What do you say?

James glanced up desperately at Helen, who made an emphatic face at him. Oh God!

'The point is that we may have an important new feature on the site', James said. 'I'm going to stick to my new strategy, the one I've just decided on.'

'You are? Well, all right then, if that's what you've decided. It's your prerogative, it's the site director's right to decide . . . Yes, I'm coming . . . Of course, it's your responsibility as well, but you know that, don't you? Anyway, I must go.'

'Well done,' Helen said.

'Helen,' James said, 'don't you ever fucking dare to plug into one of my conversations again. He knew someone was on the line, and that's bloody well going to make a bad situation worse.'

'Good, now that's more like it,' Helen said. 'At last, you're asserting yourself. The alpha administering a bit of discipline. That's better. I'm getting a frisson of scariness. But you need to be able to do it without losing your rag first. Then you might start to get a bit of respect from people.'

'Fuck off and stop taking the piss.'

He turned unenthusiastically to the remains of his lunch scattered on either side of the hateful holophone. He'd have liked to have poured himself a large glass of red wine, but Tessa might come back, and she didn't approve of drinking at lunch. What was it John Knox had said about the monstrous regiment of women? Three trumpet blasts; but sounding them here probably wouldn't be in line with policy.

Chapter 4

Uninvited Guests

Nigel's gaze dwelled on the papery thinness of Sir Trevor's skin, as the white knobbly claw that served him as a hand clutched at the stem of his wine glass. This was his second glass, and as such, the opening of Nigel's brief window of opportunity. Sober, and the old fart was perverse and intransigent. Two glasses, and he was confused and bombastic. Just at this point, the first glass downed, and the second in his hand, he might be open to persuasion, might even get fired up by Nigel's own enthusiasm.

The Lynch Bage '52 was going down well enough, and the old goat had always had a soft spot for Maria. When his attention wasn't with her, he was leering, watery eyed, across the table at Helen. They were eating out on the terrace, with the heat of the day still beating up from the ground, and the countryside fading into the half light. Maria was engaging Sir Trevor in a conversation about the local agricultural show, where a wine from one of his own vineyards had been awarded a prestigious prize. Talking about that had entertained him, while the first glass took its effect.

Helen had a bored look, and worse than that, a certain distracted air that might have made anybody, who didn't know her, think that there was something not quite right with her. If she was serious about a career in journalism, she'd have to learn to greet the boring with rapt attention. That sort of expression was a luxury that needed to be discarded with adolescence.

He glanced at the caterers, busying themselves before serving the main course. He had arranged with them that more wine was only to be served when he gave the signal. That could extend his window of opportunity by a bit, but only a bit. Sir Trevor would start to become petulant, if his glass was empty for any length of time. Right on cue, as Sir Trevor raised the second glass, Maria changed the subject.

'I'm sorry, I must be boring you with my chatter. I expect you want to tell us all about the museum. So exciting, that new wing. We're all wondering what you're going to put in it.'

Sir Trevor looked taken aback by Maria's abrupt change of subject, and not the least bit keen to talk about the museum. Eventually, he turned towards Nigel and said,

'Ah, yes, the new galleries. I'm sorry we couldn't ask your firm to join the competition. Your people only do that funny architecture. Grass and stuff on top. It had to look like the old part. We wouldn't want to develop a carbuncle, would we?'

'No, I quite understand. But as Maria said, what we're really curious about is what you're going to do with all that new space.'

Sir Trevor was chairman of the board of trustees for a major collection of Roman antiquities, and for some reason that Nigel couldn't fathom, the other trustees always followed his lead.

'Ah, well, the trustees have quite a few ideas,' Sir Trevor said.

'Such as?' Nigel asked.

'Early days, early days, dear boy.'

Maria squirmed on her seat, and seemed to become slightly slanted away from Sir Trevor. Nigel guessed that he was trying to play footsy with her under the table. His instinct was to pick him up, and throw him out of the house, but he, and Maria for that matter, expected this, and had steeled themselves for it.

'As it happens,' Nigel continued, 'I've an idea of my own. Helen tells me that this excavation down the hill here from us is turning up a lot of interesting stuff. Well, what I want to say, is that I'm prepared to offer you a state-of-the art presentation of that in your new wing.'

'Very kind, dear boy.'

'Of course, with that size of the donation, I gather it's quite normal for the new building to be named after the donor, and probably, — I don't know, have some sort of commemorative inscription, even some piece of relief sculpture.'

'Quite right, dear boy.'

'Also, I should think you could pull in a royal for the opening.'

'Hopefully, not like that duke that bored us nearly to death, opening that laboratory place, when Helen was at school,' Maria said.

'We should get what's-her-name, the fit, younger princess, the one with the good legs. That should draw a good crowd,' Sir Trevor said.

Good lord, Nigel thought, Sir Trevor had actually had a good idea. Well, Nigel's father had a theory that every fool was allowed to say one intelligent thing in their life. It was just that Sir Trevor had left his rather late in the day.

'Yes, that would be ideal,' Nigel said. 'You'd better get to work on your royal household connections. She'll be booked up way in advance.'

In his mind, Nigel saw the crowd in front of the flag bedecked portico of the museum, and himself beside the glamorous princess. He would be seen as a respected public figure and generous benefactor, an answer to all those miserable bloggers whining about him being a fat cat developer who demolished heritage buildings. He wasn't a developer, or if he was only one by accident, he was an architect, and later he'd be seen as one of the best in his period, he felt sure.

'The trouble with these Roman villas is they're just a few old tiles,' Sir Trevor said. 'We've got to fill lots of space. We have to deal with those boring people from the lottery. They say there's got to be one main theme for the whole wing.'

'This isn't just a few old tiles,' Helen said. 'It's the best surviving mosaics and Roman wall paintings in the country.'

'Helen's friendly with the guy running the dig,' Maria said.

'Yerr, well, I know him,' Helen admitted. 'I'm a volunteer down there.'

Nigel knew that Maria thought their daughter had something going with that archaeologist, although they hadn't met him yet. He wondered what he would be like. He imagined someone round and grizzled, although if Helen was taken with him, he probably wasn't round and grizzled. Perhaps a young archaeologist would be a bit dark and mysterious, liked a house-trained Dracula. Both the women looked to be uncomfortably seated now. He guessed that Sir Trevor had forced Maria to move to such an extent that she was colliding with Helen.

'The fact is, dear boy, that the trustees would like to find a home for the Cloppard, and it would take up all that space, you understand.'

Nigel had guessed this might be coming. The Cloppard was a bequest that the trustees should have refused, but were now stuck with in the basement of the museum. He recalled a succession of huge eighteenth century canvases portraying improbably large horses and other distended farm animals, all rendered in the same dingy brown colour, and set against a strange yellowish landscape. Here and there was a different style of canvas, where the sickly owners reclined on a seat, from which they viewed a badly drawn version of Cloppard Hall, as it had been in the late eighteenth century.

'But this is a Roman collection,' Nigel said. 'That's the whole purpose of your museum. The Cloppard is eighteenth century.'

'Oh, very true, very true, but you know the trustees have discretion as to any additions to the collection,' Sir Trevor replied.

'Surely the intention was to allow some discretion, for individual items, small rooms, that sort of thing, but not miles of galleries full of eighteenth century farm animals.'

Sir Trevor was beginning to look a bit bewildered. 'Dear boy, what about some more of that Lynch '52.' He was toying with his empty glass.

'In a moment. Let's get our ideas clear on this first.'

'The problem is that Lady Cloppard is always on at me,' Sir Trevor said. 'It seems a bit ungrateful not making any use of the bequest. And she's a little depressed. Having to sell the hall to that young singer. Gerald wasn't good with money, and the paintings don't have much market value, but they are a veritable time capsule, or so I'm told. Poor Gerald, didn't make old bones either. Too fond of drink and young women. It takes its toll. Of course, he was a good friend of mine at school.'

'I heard his career at your school was cut a bit short, for some strange reason.' Maria said.

'Oh, yes, I'm afraid so. Bad business. The Young Farmers' Club. What happened can't be mentioned in front of a young lady, of course,' Sir Trevor said, casting a lascivious glance at Helen's flimsy top.

'Would you speak of country matters?' Helen said.

Nigel gave her a disapproving glance. Taking the piss out of important fools would be no way to advance her future career, and not much help in the present circumstances either. Fortunately, Sir Trevor didn't seem to get her drift.

'From what I've picked up, and not to put too fine a point on it, he was expelled for trying it on with a goose,' Maria said.

'Bad business. Only the summer before, he won the prize for the most improved boy in the school. That's what got him into the Young Farmers. They were a sort of elite. I was one myself. It wasn't just anyone who could join. Had to be approved by the head master. And of course, it wasn't Gerald's fault at all.'

'The goose led him on, I suppose,' Maria said.

'It was that master's fault. The one in charge of the Young Farmers. A very slack fellow. He spent a lot of his time in the village pub. And boys of that age are very suggestible.'

Helen spluttered loudly into her napkin. Sir Trevor looked rather pained and surprised. Nigel reflected that long and expensive educations had brutally erased every last trace of feminine delicacy from both his wife and daughter. What would Elizabeth Bennett have thought of their conversation?

'A year later everything would have been fine,' Sir Trevor continued. 'There was a new headmaster, and he closed the Young Farmers on health and safety grounds. The birds had some sort of pest. Anyway, we didn't say Gerald was expelled. He was just transferred to an associated school with more pastoral care. Our place was a bit sink or swim.'

'Certainly for the geese,' Maria said. Helen was still clasping the table with a pained expression.

'I'm really getting terribly thirsty, dear boy.' There was a hint of irritation in Sir Trevor's voice.

Nigel sighed. He thought he saw his window of opportunity closing, but there was nothing to be gained from keeping the old soak dry any longer. Reluctantly, he signalled for more wine.

'The fact is, 'Nigel said, 'I don't give a toss what Gerald got up to at school, but I won't be connected with those dismal

Cloppard paintings. If you'll do this villa thing, then you've got all the funds you need.'

*   *   *

As he said this, the image of the subterranean structure they had started to uncover at the villa flashed into Helen's mind. Until now, she had been paying only intermittent attention, preoccupied as she was by the excavation, and the disturbing dreams that had come with it. Now, suddenly she grasped that there was an opportunity here. James had stressed that however fascinating their new discovery might be, there simply weren't the funds for an extensive underground excavation. But here, her father was angling to pour money into this museum. He might just as well put some of it into the excavation. Now she caught Sir Trevor saying,

'But, dear boy, the lottery people are most insistent,' Sir Trevor said, 'and I can't imagine, how we can fill even half the new wing with your villa stuff.'

'Yes, you can,' Helen said.

The other three all stared at her in surprise. 'I hadn't really updated you guys on this, but we're opening up a whole new level to the excavation right below the villa's church.'

'Church?' Sir Trevor said. 'I thought they were all heathens.'

'It was a transitional time. Anyway, we've discovered the entrance to this second underground place. Some sort of secret church.'

'Have you got inside,' Maria asked.

'Well, no.'

'So you don't know. It might just be the Roman equivalent of a broom cupboard. I really don't think the Cloppard should be dismissed as lightly as that. I look at it as an art historian. Fair enough, the paintings may not have much artistic merit. But you shouldn't just think of that. A museum is there to transmit culture through objects. Every object tells a complex story. You have to consider the social and economic context. The farm surpluses these animals represent went via the banking system to finance the industrial revolution. That, and the slave trade, of course, is what got things going.'

'Slave trade?' Sir Trevor said.

Her mother hated any idea of a link between Helen and the villa. She clearly suspected a connection to her childhood nightmares. As soon as Helen had an idea about the villa, her mother was suddenly weighing in on the side of the Cloppard, and drawing dark frowns from her father, as she did so. But, Helen could see that, luckily, her mother had made the mistake of talking right over Sir Trevor's head.

'The underground building is definitely something religious,' Helen said. 'They can tell that from the carvings on the outside wall.'

'Of course, the trustees wouldn't like anything that was mystic or too secret,' Sir Trevor remarked.

'It's probably from when the Christians were persecuted,' Helen said. Could be. She had no idea really, but it was important to stop the idiot locking on to some silly objection.

'Ah, yes. Persecutions go down well with our public,' Sir Trevor said. s.

Good, he liked the idea of persecutions. Might be a bit into sadistic fantasies

'Perhaps, I can make a suggestion,' Helen said, turning towards her father with a smile. 'The archaeology people don't have the funding to excavate much of this underground church. But daddy, if you were to put up the money, they could excavate the whole church, and probably bring up enough stuff for displays to fill this new wing. After all, there's nothing else quite like this place in the whole country. It'd be a real coup for the museum.'

Sir Trevor turned to Nigel.

'You're so lucky to have such a clever daughter. She explains things so much more clearly than you do. You must be getting old like me. Very interesting, well, anyway, I promise I'll run this in front of the trustees.'

*   *   *

Much later, they saw Sir Trevor to his car. Helen had to endure a too-tactile parting embrace, but then at last his driver was helping him into the Bentley, and finally they were watching the tail lights recede. They went back into the house. A row started to develop between her parents. Something to do with broom cupboards and the eighteenth century economy.

She went out onto the terrace to get away from it, and to finish her wine. Then she saw them. They were quite close. For the first time in her waking life, she looked on the group of people that she had seen too often in her dreams. She was afraid in a special way, felt her skin prickle and go cold, but had no notion of how long she stayed out there. Suddenly, there was a movement at her side. She glanced round, saw her mother, and then looked back at the garden. There was nothing but darkness out there.

'What's wrong?' Maria asked.

'Nothing.'

'Yes, there is. You're as white as a sheet.'

'You've been rowing.'

'Nothing unusual.'

'Perhaps, I'm drunk?' Helen suggested.

'Not particularly,' Maria replied.

'Maybe, I don't feel very well.'

'Maybe.'

Helen spotted a bottle of Cognac, reached across and poured a liberal amount into a heavy cut-glass tumbler. 'I think I'll take this up as a nightcap.'

'You don't like Cognac.'

'I do now. — Good night.'

She turned and made her way into the house. From inside, she glanced back, and saw her mother watching her curiously. Had she seen their uninvited guests as well? Certainly, she seemed aware that something strange had happened out there on the terrace.

CHAPTER 5

WHAT A TANGLED WEB
WE WEAVE

At the foot of a flight of reddish stone steps, they faced the outline of a doorway in a battered wall of the same stone.

'A pity they didn't put it under the church,' James said. 'We could have gone down through the floor. But don't take it out on me. I've warned you, haven't I? We can't possibly get in there. We'd need all sorts of specialist workers and equipment. We haven't got, and we're never likely to have the funds for that.'

'I've dealt with that,' Helen replied.

'What?'

'My father will sponsor you.'

'You didn't say anything about that.'

'I didn't want to, until things were fixed up.'

'It won't be just a few thousand. I hope he realises that.'

'He wants to redeem himself.'

'Redeem himself?'

'You know all the stuff about the Delphinium Centre,' Helen said.

'I've read something vaguely. Was he involved in that? Was he the developer?'

He tried to recall the details of a rumbling local dispute. He had an image of some charity shops and junk-food outlets in hen hutchy buildings. These had been pulled down, and replaced by a much larger structure in the modern green style, with turf roofs and turbo solar panels at improbable angles. 'Fashion Capital of the Severn Valley' — an advertisement for the project came to mind.

'He was the architect really, but they always say developer, because it sounds worse.'

'Some people don't like it. Isn't that it?'

'It's that horrid nerd group,' Helen said.

'Who?'

'Friends of the Twentieth Century,' she replied. 'They keep writing these awful blogs and things about daddy. He's supposed to have destroyed some precious heritage architecture to get his fat cat bonus. But I thought the old stuff was real crap.'

'Yes, I'm sorry,' James muttered, 'but I don't quite see the connection to our excavation.'

'It was my idea really,' she said. 'I'm quite proud of it. If he pays for the excavation, and all the bits and pieces to have nice displays at the museum, he can figure as a bit of a local benefactor. I'll get him to discuss it with you. In fact, you'd better meet both of them. Mother's being dropping hints. I think the old rumour mill's been working over time, so we can't put it off much longer.'

*   *   *

The thermometer on the side of the motor home nudged above 41°. Walking up the lane was like pushing against something tangible. He turned in at the gate of the parent's house. The first time he had been able to see it properly, half-hidden as it was by an unkempt hedge that stretched along the lane. This was another effort in the modern green style, with turf and solar panels, and windows appearing in unexpected places. Here and there, near the ground, there were outcrops of older masonry, a reminder, if any was needed, that this place had a deep past. He approached a wooden door that looked as if it might lead to accommodation for hobbits or gnomes. He pressed the bell, and heard it echoing a long way inside the house. He waited, as the heat of the afternoon pressed down on him. Then he heard footsteps and a woman opened the door.

'James?'

'Yes, — Mrs Roberts?'

'Maria. Call me Maria.' There was an awkward pause, and then she said, 'You'd better come through.' She led the way across a spacious hall with dark wood floors and Persian rugs. It was cool here, with a low hum of air conditioning in the background. Not bad for a mother, he thought, as he took in Maria.

They entered a large living room at the end of which the green turfy style had been, for a moment, discarded, to give a panoramic view of the valley. It was all there. He could see the excavation, his motor home, the site office, even, faintly, the reddish block of stone, and beyond that the village church and the field behind, where at some distant time, there had been fire and carnage.

At first, he had thought they were alone in the room, but now he realised that there was a figure crouched round a phone and a screen in a distant recess. Slowly the figure uncoiled itself, and became a very tall, well-built man. There was no mistaking his commanding presence as he approached, and then crushed James's hand.

'Nigel Roberts, glad to meet you,' the hand-crusher said.

James felt the two surveying him critically. Most likely, they were wondering why their daughter couldn't have done better for herself. And anyway, where was she?

'Where's Helen?' he asked uneasily.

'Oh, she had to go shopping with her friends,' Maria said.

What a lousy trick. Even Branwen wouldn't have pulled that one. It was just basic that it was Helen's job to introduce him.

'Would you like a glass of wine, perhaps,' Maria said.

'Yes, thank you,' he said, a bit too eagerly.

She poured one for him, but nothing for herself or Nigel, making James feel awkward. He took a sip. Good wine. Hospitable to their guests at least. Probably kind to children and animals as well.

'You can sit there,' Maria said, motioning him towards a device that looked like a sun lounger made out of some kind of glass mesh. He lowered himself gingerly on to it, and just managed to get his glass on to a small and slippery table attachment.

'I'll make you more comfortable,' Nigel said. He operated a remote control, which lowered James's seat closer to the floor, and tilted his head almost to the horizontal. He could just see Nigel's face, and behind him the sky, where a dark plume of clouds had started to grow. They could be in line for one of the ever more frequent and violent summer storms.

Maria had placed herself at a right angle to him.

'Nigel designed that chair you're on. They sell them in Kreuzers.'

'Very comfortable,' he lied.

'So you're looking for a sponsor for your excavation,' Nigel began.

'Yes, it's very kind—'

'Yes, it is,' Maria began. 'But first, we,—well, I, at any rate would, like to know what you're getting up to down there.'

'Well, yes,' Nigel said, 'but don't let's get too bogged down.'

'You must come down to see the site, when it's not so hot,' James suggested.

Sheet lightning flashed in the sky. Maria turned to look at a computer screen.

'Helen gave me some photos of the latest bit you've dug up. I'm just looking at them again here. I thought they were quite interesting. You know I teach art history'

'Yes, Helen told me.' The thunder arrived. The storm was a good way off.

'You've got chi-rho symbols carved in that stone wall.'

'Yes, typical for early Christian sites.'

'But the funny thing is the pavement in front of it. It's a bit of a mess, but I would say that's a labyrinth pattern.'

'Yes, — very common in classical art.'

'A Dionysian symbol,' she said. 'an ecstatic religion. What was supposed to happen, when you reached the centre of the labyrinth?'

'You turned towards the light. Of course religions were more intertwined, less separate in the ancient world. It's not unusual to find mixtures and overlaps of motifs from different religions.'

He reached for some wine, at an awkward angle on the table attachment. He had to raise himself on an elbow, and tilt the glass to drink from it. He miscalculated, and some of the wine slurped out of the glass, leaving him dabbing ineffectively at his damp shirt, until Maria brought him some tissues.

'You're putting James of, with all this talk of labyrinths,' Nigel interrupted. 'We ought to get on. I've got a video conference at four.'

Maria seemed to ignore Nigel.

'This is all very interesting for people like you and me,' she resumed. 'But if you were suggestible or over imaginative, it might be a bit unsettling.'

'Well—'

'One question in my mind,' Maria continued, 'is why Helen was so interested in this excavation in the first place. History was never her subject, and any exercise has always had to involve a fashionable sportswear opportunity. Now suddenly, she's happy to be covered in mud from your site.'

'Yes, that's odd,' he said, in some discomfort.

'Perhaps, I can help you,' Maria said. 'When she was a little girl, she became a bit obsessed by a bad dream. It seemed to be something to do with the Romans that had lived here. When she got a bit older, she claimed she didn't have it any more. But I've always suspected she just clammed up on us, the way children do.'

'That's just pure speculation, Maria,' Nigel put in. 'We really saw no sign of anything, since she was about eight.'

'Since your dig started,' Maria resumed, 'she's been sleeping badly. I hear her up around the house at night. Perhaps, she's told you something about these dreams and things. Look, normally I wouldn't pry, but I'm worried that she might become obsessive, unstable —.'

'No, no, she's never mentioned anything like that. I don't think so. I mean, I always saw her as very — well, — sensible.'

'You're sure of that,' she said. 'No hints dropped about something special in her interest in the site.'

'No, no, I don't think so.'

He wasn't altogether happy with his replies. He was aware of a conflict of interest. He wanted to know what was behind the red stone wall, and this sponsorship might benefit his career in so many ways. The mother was probably just being over protective, and it would be a breach of confidence to say anything, in any case. But maybe there was a risk. But it all seemed very nebulous. She was obsessed, it was true, but would further excavation do any harm, and again, they might actually make things worse by not excavating. It might turn out to be nothing more exciting than a storage cell, and the whole obsession might implode after that, although he really doubted that. The steps and the whole set up was too impressive, too monumental.

'I think you're imagining the whole problem,' Nigel said. 'Helen seems perfectly stable. I sometimes sleep badly. It doesn't mean I'm unstable.'

'Another way of looking at it, is that you're too taken up with the favourable PR of your sponsorship project, to give enough thought to your daughter's well being,' Maria said.

There was sheet lightning again, and this time the thunder was closer.

'That's unfair, Nigel said. 'The fact is I don't see a problem with Helen. Now, James, what I'm proposing is quite simple. I'll fund the excavation of any reasonably sized thing that you've got down there. All the interesting stuff, chunks of mosaic, plasterwork, whatever you found, will be housed in a new galleries attached to the museum, to be known as the Nigel Roberts Wing. There'll be a plaque with a relief bust detailing my role at the entrance. The negotiations are reasonably advanced. This is really just to put you in the picture. I hope you're happy with the idea.'

'Oh, yes. Of course. It's very generous of you.'

'Don't you think James or anyone else should be mentioned on this plaque,' Maria suggested.

'I wouldn't have thought that was at all appropriate,' Nigel said.

'No, that's not normal at all,' James hastened to agree, and then continued, 'The only thing I'm wondering about is the site here. Will you want to keep something on show here?'

'It's much too close,' Maria said. 'You must be able to see that. We wouldn't want a lot of naff people wandering round almost in the next field, and their funny little bubble cars blocking up the lane.'

'No, I suppose not—'

'Look, I've got to get ready for my conference,' Nigel said. 'It's been nice to meet you, James. We must have you round to dinner sometime, when Helen gets a break from shopping.' He came over, crushed James's hand again, and left them.

Maria kept him for a bit longer, asking questions about the site and about how he came to be an archaeologist, then when there was a pause in the conversation, he said he must be getting back to his work. Maria came with him to the front door.

'So you don't think Helen's dreams have changed much, since you started your dig,' she said as they were making their way across the hall.

'No.'

In the silence that followed, he realised he'd given both himself and Helen away. Maria was holding the door open now. She smiled and said, 'What a tangled web we weave.'

The sky lit up again, and there was a crash of thunder right overhead.

'You'd better hurry,' she said. 'We could be going to have one of those mini-tornadoes, like they had in Temple Norton last week.'

He started running once he got into the lane, but not quickly enough to avoid the onset of a fierce hail storm.

CHAPTER 6

THE MASTER BUILDERS

The tumbled confusion of the heads and limbs of broken statuary, charred timbers and shattered amphora – that detritus of dark religions and defeated cultures all flooded into Maria's mind. How they must have hated them – the ones that came after, hurling everything that they found, anything that hinted of beauty, the spirit or just the good life, into this dark hole in the ground. Afterwards, there would only be turning of earth and grunting of animals for centuries. A place for small minds with a small god assured of certain certainties. Long time before they would build anything as good as what they had destroyed.

It would have been better, if Helen hadn't kept sending her film of the ongoing excavation. Then she would not have had these images lodged in her mind. She would have only come here, after all the sad broken things were neatly boxed up, and sent away to the museum basement.

Maria looked down the steps towards the dark entry – the thing she feared – dark closed off places hidden away beneath the ground, where you could be suddenly buried, and then forgotten. Before she came out, she had told herself she was going to be strong. She'd been dreading this for more than a week, but there was no way to get out of it. Why had they had to build their church underground? What a stupid thing to do. Surely, it was just a place that people used to go to on Sundays to get bored. Why underground? She had promised herself she'd do it. She'd go down step by step, with her hands and her stomach clenched. Perhaps Nigel or Helen would take her hand. But no, she couldn't be seen to be weak. She was supposed to do it on her own. James, the new boyfriend, mustn't notice that there was anything wrong. She hadn't slept at all last night, worrying about it. And now she had that queasy, shrinking feeling that meant she wasn't going to be able to go through with it, after all. If she went down there, went in through the open door into that darkness, she might make an even worse fool of herself, by running out in a panic. Then what would James think?

Nigel was going to be angry now, and James would despise her as a silly woman, afraid, when there was nothing to be afraid of. Nigel could never understand, not since they were young. They had given up going up to London together. He would always get so angry, when she wouldn't go on that grubby toy-railway thing they had there. It was not as if he couldn't afford the express pullman buses that kept you out in the open air.

'I think, I'll stay up here, I've seen the films of it,' she said, her voice trailing away feebly into the breeze.

Nigel turned and moved closer, towering above her. He was her enemy, her critic. He was so cold. Sometimes, she would rather he would hit her, this man who could make bits of her die inside, without even raising his voice. She glanced desperately down the steps, in the vague hope of support from the others. Helen had paused and turned, already half-way down. Daddy's girl: not much help there; some people envied her having such a bright, good-looking daughter, but Maria knew she was always in second place there. James had also paused, even further down: a laggard in love, a dastard in war; well perhaps not a laggard in love, judging by the village gossip, but Nigel would have a young man like that for breakfast.

'Now don't be silly', Nigel said. 'James had it checked out by structural engineers. Clarke and Daughters, I use them myself. You're more likely to have the moon fall on your head than be buried down there.'

'It's not that. You know I don't like places like that.'

'Why've you never done anything about it? You walked out on that specialist.'

'He was an idiot, a bully. Since then, I've found out more than he'll ever know. It's a kind of short-circuit in the brain. The cure's worse than the phobia.'

'You could overcome your fear, if you really tried.'

Not this. If you ever really felt it, it would take you to a place where you didn't want to be. You'd learn something about fear, you really didn't want to know. But, I've told you that a thousand times, and you just never take it in.'

'Just pull yourself together,' he said lowering his voice to a hiss, so that James didn't hear.

'Sorry, I . . .'

'I wouldn't mind, but it isn't fair on Helen, having her mother look like an idiot.'

She felt herself curling up inside, and glanced again towards the other two.

'Daddy, stop being alpha male-ish,' Helen called back up the steps. 'You know she doesn't like these sort of places.'

'I'm a bit claustrophobic myself,' James admitted.

'You've let us both down,' Nigel hissed again. 'All right, I suppose you'd better skulk up here for a bit.' He turned a large angry back on her, and followed the other two down the steps.

* * *

Nigel had to admit that he was impressed by this subterranean working. Up above, he'd been disappointed by their tour of the excavation. He had felt a certain sympathy for Sir Trevor's assessment that Roman villas were 'just a few old tiles', and wondered how easy it would be to turn the thing into an impressive wing for the museum.

'This is remarkably well preserved, considering how little's left of the rest of the place,' Nigel remarked, his voice echoing against the Roman concrete of the domed roof.

'Yes,' James said, 'actually, the best way to preserve things is to bury them underground.'

'Strange,' Nigel said.

'Once things are out on the surface,' James resumed, 'it's a holding operation against weather, animals, agriculture and people, especially people.'

Nigel looked around at this time capsule preserved through the fourteen centuries, since enemies had stuffed earth and rubble through the open doorway. The cracked and worn flagstones beneath their feet must be much the same as when those invaders had burst in on them, and the excavators had already reopened the stone runnel that fed water to an octagonal pool.

Nigel realised that James was trying to give him an account of this place, 'It's a baptistery. The pool's deep, for total immersion—adult baptism, naked of course—the building's completely round. The Roman's had round mausoleums, and a baptistery was a mausoleum, because baptism was a form of death. I mean, you've got Biblical quotes,—what is it, erm, yes, that's it, Colossians, 2, 12, "Buried with him in baptism, wherein also ye are risen with him," and you've got the same sort of thing with Romans 6, 4, er . . .'

What on Earth was he going on about? Why did his daughter always pick such unprepossessing partners. You'd have thought she could take her pick. It had started in her teens, with the one that organised that sly garden party, one hot summer's day, while he and Maria were both out at work trying to earn enough to pay for their child's education. That was the time that Maria's precious collection of twentieth century Ikea furniture got torched to feed their monster barbecue. Then there were one or two shadowy boyfriends at university that they were never introduced to, but who didn't sound, as if they were up to much. Finally, there was the one doing the MA. They had been introduced to him, and it had taken Nigel just five seconds, to see through him as a bull-shitter. You came across so many of them in his business. Young men with not a shred of honesty or sense to their name, who tried to hustle you into projects for blocks of flats or shopping centres, in obviously wrong locations. How was it that his seeming-sensible daughter didn't see through that, and instead had to leave it to the young idiot to dump her. He'd taken that as a personal affront, having someone like that treating his daughter in that way.

Well, he supposed James was an improvement. A decent enough bloke with something that could pass for a proper job. You probably got what you saw, but it was just that he was so low-key and wimpish. Not the sort of person he would employ in his own firm, but he supposed anything did for an archaeologist.

He could hear James still rattling away in the background. '. . . early baptism was more important than now, more like the mass. The water in baptism was supposed to become the actual blood of the Christ, . . .' The man must think he was delivering a lecture to some sad group of students. Marcellus would have made mince meat of him.

Marcellus? Where did that come from? Was it something James had been saying? A Roman name? Shakespearian Roman perhaps, as in 'Enter Marcellus: "Lay on Marcellus" (clash of tinny swords) "They would have it so. Exeunt".

No that wasn't right. You had to go back, back, back down the long corridors of history, and arrive right back on this very spot. Of course, that was it. Marcellus was the master builder, the architect, the man of will, the creator of this place. The person with the will to override all the fears, the quibblings, and the demands for resources to be spent on more practical things. It was he who had the confidence, despite the slender resources of a failing kingdom, to drive deep into the earth, and to throw up this dome and its pilasters, statue niches and water courses. Nigel seemed to know why. It was a rallying point. The centre of some bizarre cult, which could serve to exhort these people against the encircling barbarians.

And now, of course, he was Marcellus's successor. The man of will, who got things done. This special and unusual building, Marcellus's building, would become the focus of the new wing of the museum, Marcellus's wing, the Nigel Roberts wing. He and this imaginary man from the past; they were the true master builders, standing head and shoulders above those around them. He could see the royal opening of the new wing, with himself enlightening the princess, as to the nature of this central feature. As architect now, he was shifting round, in his mind's eye, the possible designs that might convey the essence of this place. Visitors must be made to understand why this place was built, and the effort of will that lay behind its construction. He was beginning to visualise just how this should be presented. Suddenly, he felt a strange empathy with James, recast now as an attendant lord to Marcellus, or priest to his king, or man of learning to his man of action.

Nigel was suddenly aware of James again, '. . . St. Augustine must have been very keen to shut this place down. It would have been a real thorn in his flesh. But he didn't live to see that. Died A.D. 604. It probably took another two or three generations. I'm afraid the end looks to have been a violent one'.

'Let's go back up,' Helen said. 'Daddy's getting his vacant look.'

They climbed back to ground level. Nigel looked around, and eventually spotted the slender form of his wife, over on the other side of the site, where a number of helpers were starting to lift the mosaic floor of the villa's dining room, for transportation to the museum. The bright sun of the early morning had given way to low cloud over the hills, and there were odd spits of rain in the wind, as they crossed the site; but Nigel was walking-tall, enthralled by the project and his ideas for it. They found Maria talking to a young woman called Lizzie, who seemed to manage a remarkably pleasing fit with her jeans and T-shirt.

Maria turned a sulky and bruised-looking face to him. With the fantasy of Marcellus and the master builders, Nigel had quite forgotten the earlier spat with his wife. Now, seeing her again, he felt remorse for the hurt that he must have caused. It had always been like that, almost from the very start. They would never be properly happy now, together or apart. A sort of love survived, but laced with lots of pain. His mind went back to when they were young, and he thought that at least, she had bequeathed her looks to Helen. More was the pity that Helen didn't make good use of that.

CHAPTER 7

AT THE MUSEUM

There was fear in her stomach. Something Helen had been dreading, for a long time, it seemed. A room full of bright colours, but there were hands ushering her away from that. They were urging her down a long arcade. There were people there staring after her. Her apprehension increased. There was a somehow familiar flight of steps, and lights flickering on a dark wall. Then confusion and suddenly she's being held under water. Strong hands holding her under water, as she tries to struggle up towards a gleam of light. There were two ways to go from here. She could die. Censorina — her cousin — she died. The other way there's something else, almost as frightening. Through her struggle and terror, there's a banging sound, and slowly that seems to allow her to escape.

The door of her room opened. Her mother's figure was silhouetted against the light outside. She came in, turned the light on, and sat down on the corner of the bed.

'What is it?' Helen said.

'You had a nightmare. You were screaming. I was in my study. I heard you.'

Helen lay back feeling shocked.

'It can't go on like this, can it?' Her mother said. 'Nightmares, bad dreams, sleepless nights. James seems a nice enough young man, but this excavation may be too much for you.'

'It's nothing to do with James. He doesn't believe in . . .'

'Doesn't believe in what?

Helen didn't reply.

'Doesn't believe in hauntings and bad vibes,' her mother said.

*   *   *

As she said that, Maria's mind went back to that afternoon before Helen was even born; that moment after which nothing was ever quite right again.

After all these years, the sight of it was quite clearly etched in her memory. The crane leaning over on its side forewarned her of disaster, of lives forever upset on a summer's afternoon. Driving on round the bend in the road, she saw a red helicopter landed in the paddock, and a crowd of men in yellow jackets milling around in the lane. She recognised the foreman and some of the workers standing in a small group. Stopping the car, she tried to speak to the foreman, who turned away from her, but she managed to catch one of the younger workers. It had been instantaneous. The boom of the crane had hit two men. The helicopter had been wasting its time.

There was nothing to be done but go home; she reversed and turned in a field entrance. The initial shock started to give way to anger. From the very start, this little valley and the dark village huddled at its entrance had struck her as sinister, claustrophobic, a trap. She liked the expanses of the open hills, not these close hanging woods, which seemed always to carry a remembrance of something evil. They had been within days of exchanging contracts on her dream house, when Nigel got a tip off about this site. It was no use arguing. The great architect must seize the opportunity to build his own iconic house. Now there was a hex. People had died building their home.

* * *

Maria looked up, realising she had lapsed into silence.
Eventually she said,

'I'm not sure. There's something I've never told you. It
would annoy your father, but this place has always had a bad
feeling for me. I didn't want to come here, but your father, he
wanted to build this house, the architects own inspired design.
I suppose I married him partly because of his strength and
determination, but it can be was quite difficult to live with.
Then there was the accident. That made it all worse. Seem
the wrong thing to have done. I was seven months. Maybe
the shock, anger, resentment went on you. Yes, I've always
blamed your problems, your dreams and things on myself.'

'I don't know. I think it's more than that.'

'I think you should get away for a bit. Until this excavation
is over. Go travelling. We can let you have some money.'

'I need to concentrate on getting a job. I can't afford to
miss an opportunity. It's so competitive.'

Her mother got up from the bed.

'All right, I can see I'm not doing much good. I only wish I
could do something. Try and get some sleep. Good night.'

* * *

Helen could see that James was irritated. He had a particular
way of pushing his hair back when something was getting to
him. She had seen him doing that the day that Lizzie managed
to break that almost complete Samian dish that they had just
uncovered.

'All right,' he said reluctantly, 'Let me explain something.'

'Okay.'

'It's claimed that anything we've ever seen or read about in
any media, right from when we're very young, can resurface

in memories or dreams. That's the most likely explanation for yours nightmares.'

'It's never felt like something I'd read.'

'It can seem very real, apparently' James said.

'Certainly real.'

'You said this latest thing seemed to happen in the underground church,' James continued.

'Yes, but you never suggested anything like this happened in there.'

'I did tell you, it was probably originally a nymphaeum. A place to worship the spirits of the spring.'

'For God sake — water nymphs! This wasn't some sort of tea party for nice girls. It was a walk on the dark side,' Helen said.

'Later on,' James continued, 'when there was a church, the underground place might have been the baptistery. That seems to have happened elsewhere.'

'For christenings you mean. My friend had her baby christened. It was just some mumbling and a dab of water, and then we all went and got pissed in the Eagle. It was nothing like my nightmare. I wasn't a child, and I was right under water, I thought I might die.'

'Still the idea might have come from something you've read.'

'I doubt it.'

'What you've described is total immersion baptism. The Brits, Celts, whatever you call them did that. The lot from Rome were dead keen to stop it.'

'I have heard of total immersion, but that doesn't mean being nearly drowned.'

James made that irritated gesture again and said,

'Look, first of all, what I'm going to say now must be just between us. If this type of site gets connected to anything that sound a bit New Age, my funding will dry up. The Celtic Church has been taken on board as a New Age thing for a long time now. The reality was probably a lot less attractive, but that's beside the point.'

'I haven't got a clue what you're talking about,' Helen said. 'But all right, you have my silence.'

'There's a lot of total bollocks written about the Celtic church. I think you read, and then forgot something of the bollocks kind, and it was that which came back in this nightmare. You might have read that instead of just a quick dip, people were held under until they nearly drowned.'

'So . . .'

That irritated gesture again, and then James said,

'What you read might have claimed they were doing this to achieve some sort of altered state of consciousness. You were brought up to believe that religion was a lot of silly mumbo jumbo for the uneducated. Well, so it may be in the form we have it now, but the further back you go the more important baptism becomes as a mystery, an initiation. Mumbo jumbo or not, I suspect these people had hold of a powerful and a dangerous magic.'

Now it hit her. A powerful and a dangerous magic. She'd thought he was just bull shitting her. But that was it. Death, or something else very frightening. And real. Not a fantasy. A chill of fear gripped her. She got up, left him, went up the lane to the house, and shut herself in her bedroom.

* * *

'Are you his latest shag?'

Helen looked up to see a stocky thirty-something woman in the doorway of the motor home. Her dark hair was cut quite short, and she was wearing a grey suit.

'Well, obviously you are. Anyone who wasn't would deny it like hell. You look very young. Are you under age?'

'Twenty-five.'

'Well, I suppose it's legal, if I can believe you. That's the trouble with men as they get older. They go borderline paedophile, and only interested in the glamorous packaging, rather than anything that's inside the head.'

'Did you want to speak to James? He's out on the site, but he'll be here in a minute. Or I can phone. Can I say who it is?

'Oh, of course, you don't know who I am. I'm Branwen, I'm the ex. Oh, don't worry, I haven't come to claim him back. I wouldn't want to be mixed up with that pervert again. Well, don't give me that look. You must know what he's like. Of course, perhaps you like it like that. You look a bit smutty. Posh girls are always the worst.'

'Do you want me to get him?'

'No, you can give me some lunch first.'

'That I can't. There's nothing left. We just had a snack earlier. There's a few biscuits in the cupboard, I think.'

'Right, I'll starve then. I mean that's really great. I've had a nightmare journey. Stuck in a tunnel for forty-five minutes. Hi-Speed 6, they call it, that's a joke. They'd only give me a discount class ticket, because I've worked for the shits for less than two years. Of course, no one would work for them for longer than that. I was nearly crushed to death by a twenty-two stone teenager next to me, with a vid set that kept buzz, buzz through the entire journey. They say they can't afford business class, but that's only because the fat-arsed bastard we have for a head of department and his cronies all have to travel premium Pullman class.' Now, there's nothing to eat. Well, you could at least offer me a drink,'

Helen made a move towards the wine rack, but Branwen said, 'No, wait a moment, that stuff's probably gut rot. He's got no taste in wine. No taste or imagination with anything. But I can guess where he's likely to have tucked away something better.'

She rummaged round in the kitchen cupboards, and produced a bottle of whisky.

'Oh no, please put that back. That's a birthday present from his father. It's some special kind of whisky. He's keeping it for celebrations.'

'His father? That old toad owes me.'

With this she poured a generous measure. 'I suppose you want to know what I'm doing here. I've come for a meeting about the displays in the new museum wing.'

'But that's not here, it's at the museum this afternoon.'

'I know that. But I want to have a look at the site first. James may be trying to squeeze in some stuff that the department doesn't want. They have a fixed template for what a Roman villa constitutes. It's what goes into their itzy bitzy little film for 12 year olds. They don't want anything new or extraneous. They'd have to alter their material. That costs, and it means work, and they're too fucking lazy for that. They're not having any of this nonsense about underground churches.'

'Your department isn't funding the new wing. Why should they say what we've got to have in it?'

'We're funding half the on-going operating expenses. But you're right, some rich git is paying for the set up. But he doesn't know the first thing about archaeology. He just wants some honour and glory. He's going to be at the meeting, but he'll be happy to pay for whatever we tell him to.'

'Actually, I've got to go,' Helen said. She had to get to see her father, before he left for the meeting.

'Was it something I said? — Oh, all right, fucking be like that,' Branwen called after her, as Helen made for the site entrance.

*   *   *

Nigel had been enjoying a pleasant reverie, when his daughter rushed in. He had been examining the plans for the displays in the museum, ahead of the afternoon meeting, but from this, he had lapsed into a day dream about what it would be like when the promised princess opened the museum extension. He had just got to the point, where her limo drew up, and the famous legs emerged. Would there be a glimpse of knickers? No, that wouldn't be quite right. That would be what they'd get if they'd hired a soap star. This was going to be an up market job.

Looking up, he was mildly disturbed by his daughter's appearance. It was that wild eyed and dishevelled look that had become more and more apparent in recent weeks. Reluctantly, he was beginning to wonder whether there was some basis for Maria's worries about her. But, as soon as she started to unburden herself, he forgot about his concern for her, and began to worry about what she was telling him.

Of course, she was inclined to be naive and idealistic. That would disappear in a few years, he thought rather sadly. A project like this museum would always involve some compromises, some horse trading. But he thought he could read something sinister between the lines of her rather wild account. A life time spent in the offices of planners, developers and bankers warned him that he might be about to be stitched up by this Branwen woman.

He wasn't new to involvement with archaeology. He'd had projects in historic towns that involved archaeologists. But the discoveries had been minor, animal bones, tiles, that sort of thing. When James had shown him what they'd found, he'd had a sense that this was something big, something quite out of the ordinary run, even beyond what James was letting on to him. If it was hushed up, because for some arcane reason, it didn't suit some apparatchik, the story would gradually leak out. The truth was like water, it would work its way through given enough time, and when it emerged it could make past actions look bad. After the row over the heritage architecture, the bloggers would just love to stick the blame on him, for misrepresenting this piece of archaeology. He knew all too well the corrosive effect of blogs and net discussions, and his flow of contracts was tied to his good name. The last thing he wanted was the museum display to become a target for that type of criticism.

'I don't like it,' he said. 'We need to get this thing sorted. I won't let them mess the whole thing up. Look, I'm not fully up to speed on the ins and outs of this excavation. Could you come with me to this meeting. I would like someone of my own, who can fill in any gaps in my knowledge, if there's any sort of argument.'

'But I'm not invited. It's a formal affair.'

'I'm entitled to a PA at a meeting like that. You're my PA for now.'

Sir Trevor will be drooling over her, he's hardly likely to have her thrown out, he thought, but kept that thought to himself.

*   *   *

They were early. It was inevitable. Her father was fanatical about punctuality, and always allowed too much time. He was the sort of person who was so worried about missing a train that he got there early enough to worry about missing the one before. In the end, they had nearly forty minutes to while away. They wandered around in the museum.

She peered at a small collection of coins, really not much more than blackened discs. And then, suddenly, she was somewhere else. Some kind of arena, but now lined by stalls and little shops, while bushes and small trees grew out of crumbling banks of stone seats above and behind. The coins were in her hand. It was crowded. This was a town, but the towns were not what they once were. It was only for seconds, then she was back in the museum. Her father was staring at her.

'Are you all right, you've gone quite white,' he said.

She made no mention of her experience,

'I didn't have much for lunch. Could get something in the café?' she said.

*   *   *

Half an hour later, they were assembling for the meeting. Some kind of small library. She wondered why in such a large building, Sir Trevor had to choose such a congested room. Packing cases and some apparently homeless statues filled much of the available space, while a large wooden table and wooden chairs, both of some antique design, took up most of the rest.

'Dear girl, I didn't know you were coming,' Sir Trevor said, as soon as he saw Helen. 'Here, you must sit next to me, and cheer me up.'

Oh, God no, that means footsy all through the meeting, she thought. Sir Trevor himself settled into a large and elaborately carved chair at the head of the table. Almost immediately, she felt his foot probing her. Branwen hurried in talking all the time on her phone. She swerved a bit, as she passed the back of Sir Trevor's chair. The room was badly lit, with only one window at the far end, but Helen was pretty sure Sir Trevor had tried a low-level grope. Must like well developed arses, she thought.

Opposite her were two women, she vaguely remembered, from having been shown round the museum by Sir Trevor. Miss Bell, a tall woman with grey hair had seemed to be responsible for doing any work that Sir Trevor was supposed to do. A younger woman, Alice something, who'd strategically placed herself on the far side of the older woman from Sir Trevor, had been doing the design of the displays. Branwen went and sat next to the younger woman. On Helen's side of the table, her father was next to her and next to him James. Sir Trevor looked as if he was about to start the meeting when a small, bald man was shown into the room, and hurriedly went to sit on the far side of James.

'I'm sorry,' Sir Trevor said, 'I don't know . . .'

'Oh, I'm sorry,' her father said, 'Harold is my lawyer. I had a last moment thought that it would be a good idea if he joined us.'

'I can't think why we should need a lawyer, but if you want that it's no problem, I suppose,' Sir Trevor said.

Sir Trevor again looked as if he might be about to address the meeting, and Helen felt resigned to a lengthy and irrelevant preamble accompanied by the ever probing foot. Perhaps her father also feared the preamble, because he broke in just as Sir Trevor seemed poised to speak.

'Since you've mentioned the presence of my lawyer, I may as well come straight to the point. It's been suggested to me that the displays being planned could substantially misrepresent the villa. As a major donor, I have to be concerned for any reputational damage that could flow from a future controversy over the way this site is presented.'

'You can use your screens if you want to see the provisional plans,' Alice said. 'I've got one or two queries myself. You only show one bath house. I know there haven't been enough funds to excavate the bath house area properly, but the exploratory work suggests there might have been two, or even three, although that would be unusual of course.'

'It was only exploratory work,' Branwen said. 'I'm new to this job. But the fact is the department has a particular way it likes to have these villa sites displayed. They want them presented as working farms, part of the long-run development of this country's agriculture. They don't want them to be seen as houses for grandees. Why any normal farmer should need a sixty-room villa is beyond me, but the fact is they want the place to come over as being a farm with as few interesting frills as possible. Of course, what they want even less is for someone to come along and suggest that they had all these baths as part of some sort of cleansing ritual, and that we're really dealing with a religious site. What their plan allows is one statue of Mars or someone like that, and vague waffle about did they become Christians in the end.'

'What I'm really concerned about is the large underground structure that's apparently being ignored,' Nigel said.

'The department doesn't do underground structures,' Branwen said. 'Villas are one and two storeys on the surface. I know there's some place in Kent, but they dug that up a hundred years ago. It wouldn't be allowed now.'

'Your department may not like underground structures,' Nigel said, 'but as the major donor I want to see it represented.'

'The department's very grateful to donors,' Branwen said, 'but they don't have any input into the choice of what's displayed.'

Helen noticed her father glance down the table towards his lawyer.

'On behalf of my client,' Harold said, 'I'd like to differ with your view. My client has entered into a contract with the museum trust relative to his donation. That specifies that there will be a full representation of whatever's discovered on the villa site at Northcombe. I would draw your attention to Snodgrove v. The Ministry of Agriculture (1951), usually referred to as the Long-Horn Cattle Case. Actually, properly speaking, they were Cornish long-horned, short-tailed cattle. Some experts think they were descended from Iron Age cattle that used to roam the moors of Cornwall, but . . .'

'Harold, perhaps we can come to the point,' Nigel said.

'The point, ah, yes. Well, Snodgrove, that's Charles, the third Lord Snodgrove—they were big owners of tin mines—Snodgrove made a large donation to an agricultural museum that was partly financed by the ministry. He was a rare breeds enthusiast, and bred the said long-horn cattle—short-tailed long-horns that is, on his estate in the west of Cornwall. He was in the expectation that the museum would house a large display of material relative to the long-horns' part in the dairy industry. In particular, these cattle were at one time famous for a local cheese known as Porthloe Blue. That was in fact one of many esteemed local cheeses in production into the twentieth century, for instance . . .'

Helen noticed her father turning towards Harold again.

'Oh, yes,' Harold said, 'better move on. Anyway, for reasons that I'm afraid are lost in the mists of time, the ministry wished to limit public awareness of such local cheeses, and refused to mount the display. Snodgrove successfully sued the ministry, and obtained most of his display. I would put it to you, as the representative of your department, that Snodgrove v. The Ministry of Agriculture is a precedent in this instance.'

'I think it's a pretty open secret,' James said, 'that the legal division in your department does everything it can to obstruct the rest of you. I gather they usually say they're not going to fight a case, because they might lose, and they look to be in a good way to lose this one.'

The debate veered to-and-fro across the table. Branwen thought that her father case, if he had one, was with the museum rather than ministry. James and Branwen argued as to who had the right to determine the contents of the display. Branwen pointed out the ministry would pay half the ongoing operating costs of the museum extension.

'So what does your department plan to do if the museum doesn't toe the line,' her father said. 'The lottery has put a lot of money into the new wing. Princess Mary is booked for a royal opening next spring. What are you going to do. Start turning out the lights, close some of the galleries, or perhaps the museum's Schools and Education department. That would win you lots of plaudits. I think you'd better start negotiating.'

Branwen scowled at this, but admitted that 'those shits' had not warned her of a possible dispute over the display, or given her much authority to concede changes as to what the ministry would go along with. She did, however, fire off a warning to James that the ministry would not be promoting his theory about a Saxon crusade against deviant Celtic religious practises. He assured her that his view would be tucked away in the parts of academic articles between the introduction and conclusion that no one ever read. He suggested that the underground structure could appear as a water shrine, or something of the sort, with possible later Christian connections. Her father said the underground structure must be a central theme, but they needn't dwell on the nature of whatever cult had been practised down there.

Helen felt as if her head would burst. It was their cynicism. She felt almost ill. Branwen was a monster, but really James and her father seemed to think in the same cynical calculating way. They were striking a deal for what they could get, rather than taking any account of the truth. That buffoon of a lawyer was the only one that actually seemed interested in what happened in the past. Recall of her dreams flooded through her mind. The dreadful sensation under water, the burning buildings, the preparations for flight . . . She rose from her seat,

'You've no idea what happened there! This is nothing to do with the truth! Nothing to do with what happened there! I know that! This is just a cynical deal.'

They all stared at her in amazement. Her father took hold of her arm and hissed, 'For God sake, sit down, calm down.'

Even Sir Trevor looked taken aback, and withdrew his foot, muttering

'Dear girl, you're like me, you're not an expert.'

But it was Branwen who looked the most surprised. Helen was vaguely aware that she had taken her for someone playing at archaeology, because she fancied James, but was now surmising a hidden interest in the villa. Helen pulled her arm away from her father, and rushed out of the room.

It seemed a long time later, sitting somewhere in the museum that she became aware of the concerned faces of James and her father looking down at her.

Chapter 8

Risk Assessments

Still dark and the headlights of a car shone in at the entrance of the site. This meeting had to be clandestine, hence the arrival before dawn on a Sunday morning. It was Andrew, an archaeologist friend, but not one that James acknowledged too openly. Andrew's was senior in an organisation called 'The Gate of Remembrance' usually just referred to as the 'Gate' that researched unusual religious sites. It was not best-beloved of the academic establishment. "Going through the gate" had come to mean a loss of contact with the rational in some archaeological circles.

James was in the shower, and called out to Helen to take the key and open the gate. It was the first time she had slept over in the motor home. She liked the cosy proximity of food, beds, showers and bodies. It reminded her of the flat she had shared with her boyfriend, while she was doing her masters. Preferable to the nun-like seclusion of her room at home, the same room she'd had since she was a child.

She went out to the gate, her hair still wet from the shower. The hired bubble car drove in, and parked behind the motor home. A man got out; chubby, untidy, greying hair, but looking cheerful.

'Andrew?'

'It must be Helen.'

'Yes, he hasn't found a new one yet.'

'I'm sorry, I'm a bit early.'

'It's all right, we've got some coffee on.'

They went into the motor home, where James soon joined them for breakfast. She marvelled at the way that Andrew ploughed through the croissants that they had bought for him. No wonder he looked a bit round. He seemed to be enjoying himself, but James look worried.

'I'm sorry I had to ask you here at this time,' James said.

'No need to apologise,' Andrew replied. 'It's cloak and dagger stuff. I know I'm fringe, not respectable, pseudoscience, so the braying chorus says.'

'I wouldn't say that . . .'

'Oh, come on. I'm not just fringe, I'm well known fringe. It's wouldn't be good, if people knew I'd been on site, would it?

'Well . . .' James began, but was interrupted.

'Funding might dry up. — Professor Archibald might want to discuss longer-term career prospects.'

Once Andrew had done with feasting on croissants, they left the motor home, and walked across to the underground church. The sky was turning to a dark blue, and there was a dawn chill in the air, as they picked their way between the murky outlines of the excavation. Further down the village was still huddled in darkness. Uphill in the other direction, Helen could see a solitary light in her own house. It was in her father's office, of course. Typically there before day break. Beavering away, wanting to be larger than the other beavers, king of all the beavers. He would never stop, never rest, driving himself and others onwards.

Once they had entered the lower church, Andrew gazed around in silent wonder, examining with close interest the domed ceiling, the pilastered niches and most of all the octagonal pool of water in the centre.

'Marvellous. I've dreamt, we'd find something like this. I was sure there were things like this hiding away, but it's putting your hand on them. How did you do it? Good geophysical survey?'

'Hm . . . that and the location of multiple bath houses, and elements in the upper church,' James said

'Well, not really,' Helen objected. 'I had to force him to do it.'

'That's not quite true. All right you had an idea, but I had to take stock of the hard evidence.'

'Believe me, Andrew, it was 90% or more from me.' Helen said crossly.

'I didn't realise you were an archaeologist,' Andrew said.

'No, I'm not.'

'So, how . . .'

'Don't ask,' James said.

'You two have secrets from me?' Andrew's expression was amused.

'A dream,' James half mumbled.

'Okay, I don't go there. Perhaps I should have left you with your secrets.'

'I thought you were, interested in the off beat,' Helen said.

'There's fringe and fringe,' Andrew replied. 'Dreams constitute "and fringe". My organisation was named for a famous scandal to do with something like that, but actually worse, early in the last century; The Church of England owned the site. Bit of a sense of humour failure, when they found out what had been going on.'

'That archaeologist was banned from his own site, if I remember rightly,' James put in.'

'True. But we don't go there now, we have bulwarks against the dark tide of the occult. We're unpopular enough as it is.'

'But you are impressed by this place,' James said.

'More than that. It's a gift. A keystone. I'm convinced there's a chain of these villas used as religious centres.'

'In this country?' Helen asked.

And all round the fringes of the old empire, beyond the reach of close religious control. But apart from Lullingstone, and that's only small, this is the first one that's been properly uncovered.'

'What makes you so sure there are others?' Helen said.

'I've had tip offs about things being quickly covered up again, because they didn't fit with theory. Hindley Grange, further north from here, it happened there, and there's two more in Brittany and one in Galicia, I'm pretty sure of.

'Not what they'd call statistically significant,' Helen said.

'No, but extrapolating from those, you can see similar lay outs and similar caches of religious items in a lot of other places, at least one not far from here. I bet there's dozens of them if only we could excavate.'

'But you can't,' James said with a hint of gloomy resignation. The early morning didn't suit him, but Andrew's plump form stilled glowed with the enthusiasm of the moment.

'You should join us,' Andrew said.

'Join you? You mean your 'Gate of Remembrance' people. I'm not mad.'

'You don't need to be mad,' Andrew said. 'I bet you're hamstrung, as to what you can say and do about this.'

'That's true,' Helen put in quickly. 'There was a row at the museum the other day. They wanted to leave the underground bit out. They seem to have conceded a bit, but it's all going to be very dumbed down, and . . .'

'Helen . . .' James tried to interrupt, but was ignored except for a scornful glance.

'And poor James has promised that his famous Saxon crusade theory can only be mentioned in the parts of articles that no one reads apparently.'

'Helen, that whole discussion was confidential.'

Andrew gave a slight laugh. 'So more secrets from me, I thought we were friends. Together in this.'

'We are, of course. But — well, you must be able to see how damaging it would be if this stuff started to get into public circulation.'

'Your secrets are safe with me,' Andrew said, 'but what Helen says confirms my point that you'd be better of working with the 'Gate', working with people who think along the same lines.'

'Better off is what I wouldn't be, not in the longer run at any rate. It's just too risky.'

'You should learn to take risks,' Helen said. Because you won't take risks, they can give you the type of crap that you got in the museum.'

'You don't know what you're talking about.'

'I know exactly what I'm talking about,' Helen replied. 'You're someone who actually had an original idea. Didn't just copy something for a fashionable authority on the subject. But you don't have the guts to follow it through. You're weak. You let yourself be bullied out of what you really believe.'

'I got the go-ahead to excavate this site,' James responded. 'That was more difficult than you might imagine.'

'All right, I suppose someone has to pay for your excavations. But now Andrew's people are offering to do that.'

'There speaks a rich kid,' James said. 'You've never had to worry where the money was coming from.'

'James, you need to adjust to your new social milieu,' Andrew said. 'Branwen had one of the best minds I've come across, and she was volatile to say the least, but underneath she was a daughter of the common people with her feet on the ground. Now you're mixing it with public school girls. They don't think disasters going to fall on them if they take a dodgy job.'

'I never used to like public school girls, James said. 'They gave the impression of owning the world.'

'I'll let you into a secret,' Andrew said. 'They do own it.'

'And they can't cook.' James was ignoring Helen's darkening expression.

'Nor could Branwen,' Andrew said. 'From what you used to tell me, she regarded food and drink as convenient missiles.'

'I'd really rather you didn't drag the ex into this,' James said. 'And anyway, it's not much use her having a good mind, because she's gone over to the dark side.'

'What?' Andrew said.

'I mean she's joined the bureaucracy. The control freaks. The idea stranglers.'

'I hope you two enjoy taking the piss,' Helen said. 'I take this seriously.'

'And so do I,' James said. 'Just try and stretch your tiny mind. You know what happened when I was young. I've told you my parents saw it like a miracle that I got something relatively secure. They'd think I was insane, if I told them I'd given it up.'

'Oh now comes the hard luck story, about poor James as a child,' Helen said. 'The parents' bungalow or hut, or whatever it was, repossessed when he was nine. The parents redundant seven, or was it seventeen times, between them? And the pathetic worry each time in the supermarket, waiting to see if the credit card would bounce in front of a queue of people.' She stopped. She could see he was registering pain, and suddenly she felt as if she was kicking something that was helpless.

After a silence, Andrew spoke, although he was no longer buoyant, but looked rather wary, as to what effect he might have.

'If I can put in a few words, it might not actually be so risky now. Things have changed at the 'Gate'.

'Changed? How?'

'The new fund-raising woman, I told you about. We never used to do much about that. Just bumbled along with the founders' endowments. She's managed to tap into billionaires around the world. Some people are overjoyed at be able to back this sort of excavation. It's amazing the sort of money that's out there. What we lack now are professional archaeologists like yourself.'

'For good reason, there's no more career after working for you.'

'You shouldn't need one,' Andrew replied. 'We can pay more than you're getting now. You could probably retire early.'

'So not such a big risk,' Helen said.

'You've no idea,' James said. 'This woman and her billionaires could piss off at any moment, leaving me without a job.'

'Excuses, excuses, If you were serious about your theory, if you were going to get anything done in life, you'd just walk away from all that shit we saw at the museum.'

James didn't reply. He glanced from Andrew to Helen and back to Andrew and looked trapped.

'Well, think about it,' Andrew said. 'The offer remains open. I know it would be great to have you on board. It doesn't sound like much joy, where you are at present.'

'Forget it. He's too scared to think about anything except his next salary payment and the ones after that stretching into infinity and the grumpy-old-man pension even beyond that. I can't take this. Andrew, I'm sorry, I'm going.'

She left them, left the site and made for home. It was like that time in the museum all over again. Her head felt like it would burst with frustration. James had a real idea, but he wouldn't go after it. And there was the other thing. They seemed sometimes to be on the edge of understanding all this shit in her dreams, and nowadays it was worse than dreams. Yet he wouldn't help her there. She should dump James. She couldn't respect him. Yet at the same time, she knew she couldn't do it. Something bound her to him, something not meant to be broken, inspite of all the times he disappointed her.

Reaching the house, she went to her room and flopped down on the bed. Staring upwards through the window at grey expanses of sky, ideas twisted and twirled in her mind, becoming in time more exotic. She thought she saw there was a way to get to the bottom of what had been going on here. It was dangerous. She really might die, but she was tired of this stuff.

She'd need help. She couldn't do it by herself. That was a problem. But then she knew just who could help her. They owed her. They'd bored her for enough years, and there was still a lot of things that she did for them. Angela and Margaret, they'd be ideal. They'd stuck to her like burs all these years, now they could earn their keep, or if they didn't, it would be a blessed excuse to severe the connection.

Her mind went back to her first day at university. Rather frightened and lonely, although she hadn't liked to admit it even to herself. Back at the bottom of the pile again, after being one of the senior ones marked out for a good university. And then she spotted a girl that she had never spoken to, but vaguely remembered from parties back home. She went over and that was Angela. Next to Angela was the even less grabbing Margaret. Their circles diverged after the first few weeks, but she had lacked the ruthlessness to shake them of, especially as they were almost neighbours at home. Now she could be rewarded for putting up with them.

CHAPTER 9

DANCE OF MAENADS

'No, no way,' Angela said.

Helen was perplexed. She wasn't used to resistance here. They were always so glad to tag along, whenever she suggested something. She glanced towards Margaret, who was thumbing through the pages of a fashion magazine. No help there. Margaret wasn't exactly an executive type of person. She would leave it to herself and Angela to resolve this.

'I'd do it for you.' Helen's tone was a bit cross, and as she said this, she wasn't sure that she actually would, but then Angela owed her.

'Then you'd be mad.'

'I've looked it all up. Zero risk. Not with someone young and healthy. You just have to keep a watch on the time.'

'You can't rely on that. There's always variations. People with unexpected weaknesses.'

'Anyway you've done first aid. You could revive me,' Helen said.

'I did bandages and checking blood flow. I don't know much about people with their lungs full of water.'

'It'd never come to that.'

'It might. And then we have to explain to your parents and the police that we held you under water until you were dead.'

'Well, if the worst came to the worst, you could just leave me there.'

'Fuck that. It's not going to be just a casual "wonder what happened to her". There would be a mega fuss, and they're be bound to track down the fact that we were around when it happened. God, Helen, this is nonsense. We're absolutely not getting involved. It's totally bizarre.'

'I'd be too frightened,' Margaret said.

Helen realised that was the final word. Margaret went through life looking for an authoritative view on everything from Plato to fashions in shoes, rather than bothering to think about anything for herself. Once she had her authority, she would defend it come what may. This time she had clearly adopted Angela as her mentor, so, it was going to have to be plan B.

In a way Helen was quite relieved. Inspite of what she had said to Angela, plan A was quite frightening, while plan B was just a bit of fun. She described plan B, and both the girls nodded willingly, looking glad to fall back into line with her wishes. She left out one element of plan B, but there was absolutely no reason why the other two should know anything about that. Tom should be able to get her what she needed.

* * *

James cursed to himself. He'd left the papers he needed in the site office. It was well past midnight. He was tempted to call it a day, but reminded himself of his resolve to finish his report. He stepped out of the mobile home heading for the office. A fine summer night; the moon full and low down in the southern sky, and here far from the lights of towns, the stars were visible above his head. He stopped for a moment to take in the scene, and then there was something incongruous. The sound of music; not the noise of some distant rave, but a slow persistent music like flutes somewhere close. Intruders? The only gate onto the lane was padlocked with barbed wire on top. A dense, high hawthorn hedge ran along the lane, while barbed wire fencing and scrappy hedgerows marked the boundary with fields on the other sides. Should he investigate? He wasn't a security guard, and on a Saturday night it would difficult to get police to a break in at a ruin. Nevertheless, he didn't feel he could just leave it, and there was an element of curiosity.

He made his way into the middle of the site. It seemed to him that the music was coming from somewhere near Helen's house, and he picked his way cautiously in that direction. As he did so, he became aware of a faint glimmer of light and the music became louder. Reaching the hedge at the boundary of the site, he could still not make out what was going on. He crept cautiously along the hedge, until he reached a point where only a cattle trough separated the site from a paddock belonging to Helen's house. The paddock was the former residence of a now defunct entity known as "my old pony" or alternatively "that right stroppy bastard".

Crouching behind the cattle trough, he was not a little surprised by what the flickering light of candles revealed in the paddock. Helen was there. She was dancing to the flute music, and wearing a long white garment, probably meant to look like something Greek or Roman, with a metal clasp at the shoulder. With her were two girls, stark naked, and also dancing to the music with flutes in their hands. After a few moments, he realised they were just miming, and that the music came from a small device with a blue light placed on the ground between the three dancers. He recognised Helen's companions. They were two rather plain girls that she had brought one day to see round the site. He had suspected that they attached themselves to Helen in the hope that she would help them pull. That said, the naked buttocks and thighs of the girl nearest to him were vaguely arousing as she gyrated in the candle light. The other one had begun to spread a bit, which spoiled the effect. Really, he ought to get back to his work. It was nothing to do with him, what they got up to in Helen's paddock, but instead he remained gripped by curiosity as to where this was going. At the same time he was uneasily reminded of the story of some Greek king, who was torn to pieces after being caught watching women's rites.

After a time the tempo of the music increased, and some eerie metallic clashing, cymbals perhaps, joined in with the flutes. Helen reached for the metal clasp at her shoulder and the white garment dropped to the ground; nothing underneath; a bit of a shock despite being used to seeing her like that. She threw her head back, writhing more than dancing now, looking almost as if she was close to orgasm. One moment she was like that and the next she was spread-eagled on the ground, still and silent. The other girls ran forward, and then stopped, seemingly uncertain what to do next. Realising he could not remain concealed, he scrambled into the cattle trough, first one and then the other leg sinking through cold water into some kind of sludgy slime.

'Who's that?' Angela called out in alarm.

'It's James, I heard your music,' he said by way of excuse, as he levered himself out of the cattle trough.

He went across and looked at Helen. No sign of movement or sound at all, and deathly white.

He glanced across at Angela and said,

'Do you think she's dead?'

'I think she's breathing, but we'd better get her back to the house. Can you carry her?'

James looked down at Helen's long, sprawling limbs. He had a vague notion that a man should be able to carry a woman, and he was quite assiduous in the gym, but still he couldn't see himself getting her back to the house, if indeed he could lift her at all.

'No, you two take her legs, and I'll go at the front,' he said.

They lifted her and started to stumble their way across the paddock. All the time, as he moved backwards over uneven ground and tussocks of grass, he was afraid of falling and dropping Helen.

'Look where you're going,' Angela advised.

'I can't, you look out for me.'

'Well turn round, you idiot.'

'No, this is the best way to hold her, she's bloody heavy.'

'You don't need to tell us that,' Margaret put in. 'I can't fucking keep going much longer.'

'You've bloody well got to,' Angela told her.

At last they reached the end of the paddock and from there managed to enter the garden of the house. James thought they were almost there, but he hadn't reckoned with Nigel's ideas on garden design combined with the enclosing darkness of the house and a tall hedge. They descended a flight of steps that looked like the one's leading to the front door, only to find themselves by a small ornamental pond.

'You idiot,' Angela said.

'How do we get out of here?' James looked in vain at stone walling and rockery plants on all sides, as Helen's weight continued to tug on his arms.

'The way we came in, it's the only way,' Angela replied.

James' muscles were burning, and Margaret was moaning and cursing her companions, as they extricated themselves from the pond area. James stumbled against a cunningly placed decorative stone and nearly dropped Helen head first onto a stone path. But just after that he was relieved to hear Helen moan. At least, she was alive and conscious.

'We can't stop, we've got to get her indoors,' Angela said.

At last the right set of steps emerged from the darkness of the garden, and they made their way down to the front door. James lowered Helen gently to the ground and said,

'Let me have the key.'

This request was followed by an awkward silence.

'Well, one of you must have it,' James said. There was another slight moan, but nothing more from Helen.

'Helen . . .' Angela said.

'Is it in the paddock?' James asked.

'I don't think there were any pockets in that thing she was wearing,' Angela said.

James glanced at the door bell, and back at the two girls. There seemed to be a tacit acknowledgement that confronting Nigel and Maria like this would not be a pleasant experience, but there didn't seem to be much alternative, until Margaret suddenly said,

'I think there was something on her wrist.'

Angela bent down, discovered the key, and gave it to James. As soon as he opened the door a series of brilliant lights sprang on throughout the central hall of the house. Then, as soon as they had manoeuvred Helen through the front door, it swung to with a loud bang, further confounding any hopes of a surreptitious entry.

The hall reached up through the first floor to the roof space, and extended for some way to the left of the front door. Stairs ran up from the centre of the hall to a balustraded landing. There was a large leather sofa placed along the wall to the right of the door. Exhausted, they deposited Helen on this, and covered her with a rug that had been hanging on one arm of the sofa.

'James, could you get some water,' Angela said. 'She may be dehydrated.'

'Where . . . ?' He was confronted by a series of identical wooden doors on the far side of the hall. They both glanced at Margaret, but she was leaning against the door, crying, and tried to cover herself with her arms, when she saw James looking at her.

'Oh, for God's sake,' Angela exclaimed. 'I'll get it. You keep an eye on her.'

As Angela was on her way back with the water, they heard a door opening in the upper part of the house. A moment later, Maria was coming down stairs, quite striking, with her dark hair dishevelled and wearing a blue Empire style night dress.

'Helen fainted,' Angela said. 'She was dancing, and just fainted.'

Maria's surveyed the nakedness of the two girls before saying,

'Something pagan'

'Er . . . not . . .'

'Just dancing in the nude for the hell of it?'

'Something to do with the villa. The excavation,' Angela said.

Maria's glance fell on James,

'Your idea, I suppose?'

'Oh, no,' Angela said. 'He was just spying on us.'

James saw the ghost of a sarcastic smile flit across Maria's face, and then Angela said,

'Helen wanted to contact some people to do with the villa.'

'People?'

'People who used to live there, I think.' Angela looked uncomfortable.

'Dead people?'

'A bit . . . er . . .'

'A bit dead?' Maria suggested.

'A bit like that.'

'And you were going to do this by dancing?'

'Er, . . . we had a glass of wine first.'

'Not just wine, I suspect.'

'Er . . . I don't know.'

'No?'

'Helen started seeming a bit odd after hers.'

Now to his further dismay, James saw the huge shape of Nigel, clad in a vibrant tartan dressing gown, advancing down the stairs. Was it the Campbell tartan, the ones that did that massacre in history? He wasn't sure. Maria also glanced up at him, and then told the girls to get some coats from a cloak room off the hall. They went in and shortly re-emerged with white legs poking from under two of Nigel's capacious jackets. Maria turned to Nigel as the tartan monster advanced across the hall and said,

'Helen fainted. She's all right now, but I was right about what's been going on with her.'

James saw Nigel contemplate first the ashen face of his daughter as she sipped some water, and then the bare legs of the two girls, before saying to him, 'And I suppose you organised this, whatever it was?'

'No, apparently he was just spying on them,' Maria said.

'Not a stain on your character then — well, hardly,' Nigel said.

'We can talk about all this in the morning,' Maria said. We don't need to move her now. I'll stay down here and keep an eye on her. The rest of you'd better get to bed.'

James saw Nigel's glance focus on the slimy and now beginning to be foul smelling mess that the cattle trough had left on his legs. He backed against the door as the tartan beast moved closer to him. He loomed over James, tilting his chin slightly upwards, as if disdaining the idea of addressing him directly,

'Looks like it's time to get back to your little camper van,' Nigel said.

'Oh, right, yes, I'd better be going,' James muttered. He slid along the door, opened it, and slipped out into the night.

On the way back down the lane, he could only wonder how he had managed to be left looking so foolish. It was just chance that he had happened to step outside and hear their music. Having heard it, it was only natural to find out what was going on. After that, well, who wouldn't have been curious to know how things were going to develop. In the event, it had been fortunate he was there to help get Helen back to the house. But at the end of the day, he was the one who ended up looking a complete fool, and a bit of a pervert as well.

*   *   *

It was a summer's day. She was younger — sixteen. Sitting on the grass. Banks of flowers and herbs with the white stucco of walls behind them and the orange of pantiles above. A fountain sparkled and splashed in the sun. Helen thought she knew this place. Somewhere that might have been frightening to her once, but not now. She was with friends, laughing and talking. Censorina her cousin and her best friend was here. She had seen her arrive on her white pony. But that was strange. She felt a chill. She thought that Censorina had died. She thought she knew that. But that was silly, because here she was sitting out her on the grass with the rest of them, looking perfectly healthy, and braiding her beautiful hair.

Helen followed a tiny white cloud as it drifted high up across the blueness of the sky. It amused her because she thought it had the shape of a little pig. But then at the back of her mind she had the awareness that there were larger, darker clouds. Sometimes she saw her father and some of the other men in conclave after dinner, looking worried. She knew that there were enemies away to the south and east.

Then she saw that young priest, the one who always seemed rather keen to talk to her, passing just on the far side of the fountain. Heading towards the church. That was a second cloud. There was another, secret place beneath the church. Once there had been spirits of the water there, but then the true god came, mighty and fearful. The reason why this place was important was that secret place. Something that made them better than their enemies. Something their enemies wanted to do away with. She thought that she might soon become part of that secret — that Censorina already had.

*   *   *

There was a pain in her head and her throat was dry. Helen felt a glass being pressed between her lips, and she spluttered as the water went down. She managed to open her eyes. How did she get here, back in the house, when she should have been outside. It was a muddle of concerned faces. James was here. That didn't make sense, why did he appear everywhere? Now her parents. How had everybody got involved like this. She shouldn't have trusted Angela and Margaret that was a mistake. They were a couple of useless prats.

But through her discomfort and confusion, she knew she had arrived at understanding. It used to be a matter of nightmares, even perhaps haunting. But now she wasn't afraid any longer. She had seen it the way it had been, and knew that it wasn't anything evil. This had been a special place. They had found it again after all this long time, and no one should be allowed to hide it from the rest of the world.

CHAPTER 10

THIRTY PIECES OF SILVER

Something was disturbing the carefully ordered avenues and pathways of Nigel's life. He prided himself on achieving what he had, while remaining the model family man. Someone in his position got plenty of hinted offers and opportunities, but he had succeeded in remaining faithful to Maria. Not for him the graduate trainee on the boardroom table or in the broom cupboard, nor the blow job from the young accountant on the stairs to the plant room. Still less the suspiciously repetitive and exact 200 Asian dollars room service on the corporate credit card, courtesy of the Hotel of the August Moon, Saigon.

And he had made time for Helen, where others might not have done. Taken the carbon-premium helicopter costing more than an honest worker would make in a couple of months, to be in time for the school play. They had brought up the model daughter, or so he had thought. Perhaps there should have been a sibling, a second child. That would have rounded off the picture of domestic bliss. But Maria had if-ed and but-ed until one day the opportunity had slipped away. He was faintly aware that for reasons he could not quite pin down, Maria had sometimes not seemed quite as happy as he would have hoped when they were younger.

But the thought of a lack of domestic happiness brought him back to the scene he had witnessed the other night. Those girls naked in the hall, his daughter lying ashen-faced on the sofa and that young archaeologist, whom he was coming not to trust. Reluctantly he admitted that for once Maria had been more aware than himself. There was some sort of problem with Helen. What had seemed to him the faintest rumble of summer thunder was now lightning close at hand. Still all this talk of dreams wasn't really the core of it. What Helen needed was a proper job. That would soon take her mind off whatever bad events might be hinted at in the ruins of that villa.

It was partly his fault. Well, not his fault, but his slight miscalculation as to how things would turn out. When she had finished her masters, he had given her quite a generous allowance to tide her over. He had imagined she would easily find a job in a month or two, and he didn't see it as his place in life to have a daughter constrained by poverty. But now they had cycled over a year, and still no sign of a job.

Perhaps he had made life too comfortable for her, so she could drift on in a limbo of one day becoming a journalist. Could she become a Carnchester child, a syndrome his neighbours sometimes talked about, referring to a village that had acquired the unenviable reputation of being a place where indolent adult children lived off the indulgence of affluent parents. He didn't really think that. Helen had always been so ambitious, but it was open to anyone to become a lotus eater given the right conditions. The upshot was that he was going to have to talk to her about her future.

That sounded easy, but he had to be careful how he chose his time. It had to be when the archaeology wasn't on, and when Helen wasn't rushing to see a friend, and also preferably when Maria wasn't around, because if she got wind of their chat, she would side with Helen, and say why shouldn't she take a long time to find a job. She hadn't bought the idea that Helen's problem was the lack of a job. Come to think of it, Maria was a bit of lotus eater herself. No, well, that was unfair, but he suspected that if he had made less money, she would have gone the extra mile to make herself a head of department at her college, or moved somewhere else to get promotion. He reflected for a moment on the thankless aspects of being a parent, called in to deal with things when they went wrong, while the rest of the time they were off having a good time with other people. Just then, he heard Helen in the hall. Actually, this was an ideal moment. It was a Sunday, and Maria was at a charity lunch for something to do with walruses.

'Helen . . . er . . . I wonder if we could have a word.'

'I'm meeting some of the crowd at the galleria.'

'Um, it won't take very long. You could always phone to say you'll be a few minutes late. It's just I think we need to have a bit of a chat.'

She hung her head slightly, but came into his work room without making any further comment. She plonked herself down on the edge of the sofa in a tense position, supporting herself with her arms rather than sitting back. He took the large arm chair next to the sofa. She glanced at him cautiously and said,

'I made a bit of a fool of myself the other night. Sorry about that but . . .' Her voice trailed away.

'Um . . . that's not really what I wanted to talk about.'

There was a moment's silence, before he continued,

'I think you need to think about what you're going to do for a job.'

'Er . . . yes.'

There was a further silence until he said,

'Well, you've been a year now without finding anything, — in journalism I mean. You must have thought about alternatives.'

'I'm working on the journalism. I nearly got that thing at the *Cybertiser*. If it hadn't been for that bloody girl . . .'

'What?'

'Oh, never mind.'

There was another silence. 'I mean, of course, this is your home. It's very nice to have you here, but the present set up — it's not really a way of life.'

A slight flush came to her cheeks and she said,

'Don't think I've just been sitting here. I've been scanning everything for jobs, trying everything. Do you think I want to become a Carnchester child?'

'Oh, no, no, of course not, I didn't mean that at all. It's just that it can sometimes happen that what you want doesn't want you. I've had to give up projects sometimes. Things that looked absolutely right for our company, but the potential client didn't see it that way. They wanted something else, and sometimes they suffered for that, but that didn't do me any good.'

She stared at him silently. He suspected that this difficulty with the journalism job had come as an unexpected blow to her. She'd gone through life unopposed, doing well in schools and universities, possessed of looks and security. Perhaps her relationships had been more turbulent. That was a dark area of which they only saw glimpses. He felt he should soften the blow a bit,

'You've tried going it alone? Just putting up your own stuff?'

'Yes, but there so many out there. You really need to be part of something that has a name. I mean if you want to make a proper living. It's all right for hobbyists.'

'Maybe, you need to specialise in some area that's less competitive.'

'Er . . . perhaps . . . I mean . . . are you thinking of anything in particular.'

He wasn't, but suddenly a thought came to him, 'Archaeology, perhaps. That always gets a lot of interest from the media.'

He saw she was surprised that he'd thought of something that perhaps should have occurred to her.

'Otherwise, perhaps you should start to think of something else.'

She flopped back onto the sofa. Her expression was sad and worried.

'Like what? The two-year course will have been wasted if I do something else.'

'Some of your friends went into the City or the law. Perhaps you should think of something like that. Wasn't it Jo who got into some top City firm?'

'Schlacher Sisters. But she's out of work now.'

'How did that happen? She always struck me as a capable sort of girl.'

'She is, but Schlacher cut 30% of their staff every year. She had two good years, but then her team were involved in something that went belly up apparently.'

Thirty percent. Surely that was no way to run a business. He was the last person to carry passengers, but that was going to the ridiculous opposite.

'Have you ever thought of working for me? I'd quite like to pass something of the business on in the family.'

She shook her head. The suggestion looked like it came as a complete surprise. Yet he had often thought of the lack of an heir, and that what he had built would in not so many years melt into something else or into nothing at all. But she had been dedicated to the idea of journalism since watching a programme about an investigative journalist at the age of twelve.

'And you wouldn't think of it now?' he said when no further reply came.

'I'd have to train as an architect. I'd be nearly thirty. And you need maths. It was my only bad subject at school. I could never see the point of it. $x=y^2$ and that sort of thing, and maths teachers always try to take the piss about how superior maths is. But I suppose it stops your buildings falling down.'

'I didn't mean you being an architect. Frankly, architecture is the least important part of the business. What's needed is lots of educated-type glad handing of clients, planners and media. Too often if the client is allowed to cut through to the actual architect, they decide that that person isn't impressive and go elsewhere, probably to a complete charlatan.'

'I see — well — possibly.' She sat upright again and turned towards him. 'Look, I have got a promising interview. Something really interesting.'

'Oh, who?'

Dark Star.

'Them. Really. The only ones who admitted to liking the Delphinium Centre.'

'Yes. It's really just one bloke and some chosen free lance contributors.'

This played into his hands. He'd been meaning to give her three months to find something before putting her under any pressure, but now he said,

'All right. See how that goes. If you don't get it, perhaps you could try out a few weeks as a trainee in our office. Even if it doesn't work out, it's something to put on your CV.

'Yes, I suppose so — okay.'

'Our new recruits usually simulate greater enthusiasm.'

'No, really, sorry. I didn't mean it like that. It's just a complete change of direction.' She glanced at her watch and jumped up, 'God, I'm so late. They'll wonder where I am. I'm sorry, I can't waste any more time.' With this she hurried out of the house.

*   *   *

Helen could see was drinking in the last-chance saloon. If this Dark Star interview didn't work out her life scheme since she was twelve would fade into nothing. She was apprehensive of her father's suggestion. She didn't know anything about the business, nor did she like the idea of being the bosses daughter brought in because she hadn't been able to make her own start in life. She didn't blame he father for running out of patience, and of course the other night hadn't made things any easier. It was so frustrating. She'd done well in her masters. Nothing in her whole career suggested she was unsuited to journalism. Others on the same course had got the sort of jobs she was aiming for, without appearing to be outstanding.

Searching around for reasons for her failure, Helen thought of talking to her old supervisor, Greta Clayton. It had taken her a while to get round to Greta, because between her and Greta there had always seemed to be, for no very apparent reason, a certain froideur. She had never been able to explain that. Perhaps she had picked up from somewhere that her father was a property developer, not an architect but a property developer. That could make one a bit persona non grata in a lot of places. The other seemingly remote possibility was that she had been jealous of Helen's looks. Some of her friends said she was beautiful. She couldn't see it herself. When she was eleven, she had overheard her grandmother saying to her aunt that it was a pity she was "a big gawky thing", and that had fixed her self-image for good. Her ideal was to be small and blonde with rosy cheeks and a curvy figure, whereas the reality was something like the opposite of these. James was what you'd call reserved. He'd really never referred to her looks, only to clothing if something was revealing or figure defining. As for Dick, her boyfriend during her masters, he only ever seemed interested in what he referred to as her 'pert arse'.

But the fact remained that desperate times demanded desperate measures, and that had to include contacting Greta. Perhaps whatever reservations she had had about Helen had been forgotten in the year since they had last met, or perhaps Helen had imagined it all along. With these thoughts, Helen dispatched a message to Greta, asking for advice on jobs and interviews. She waited more than a week for a reply, by which time, it was the evening before her interview with Dark Star. She was beginning to think that Greta would not give her even the courtesy of a reply. But at eleven that evening she at last picked up a response:-

Helen,

I've been extremely busy preparing new course material. This is a very busy time of year in my job, and it is only now that I have had time to respond to your mail.

You mention that you performed well in your masters, and find it disappointing that you have not to date found what you would regard as a suitable job. In this respect, I think you have to appreciate the difference between the academic grounding and suitability for the actual profession. Journalism is a matter of flair, and I doubt that you really have this. I have to say that I also found your way of treating material rather superficial. You might think that this suits you to the more popular areas of journalism. However, in these you need conciseness and an ability to express yourself with a simple vocabulary. Your own style of writing is rather literary, and can involve long and unusual words, perhaps intended to impress your readers. Charming in its way, but unsuited to the cut and thrust of the modern profession.

You mention that several of the other people on the course have found very good openings. In most cases, they were helped by my recommendation, which as you can imagine carries considerable weight, and certainly helped these candidates against the very tough competition you always get in this profession.

Your best prospect might be to look for openings in specialised areas such as hobbyist magazines and blogs, where the work may involve more of a catalogue of facts and events, requiring less flair from the writer. However, the rather literary basis of your education, if I remember correctly, might leave you struggling with these harder factual areas.

I am sorry not to have been of more help to you in your present situation. It only remains for me to wish you every good fortune in your search for employment.

Kind regards
Greta Clayton

Helen was angry in a variety of ways after reading Greta's letter. She was angry with herself for being so naive as not to guess that some of her peers, who had been successful with jobs, had been running on an inside track. She was angry with Greta for setting up something that excluded her, and even more for what she saw as a pretence that she lacked some sort of mysterious flair possessed by Greta's chosen. She was also at a complete loss to think of any long and unusual words. Pretty clear all this talk was just a screen for Greta's dislike of her, which itself had no rational basis. The effect of the letter was the opposite of what Greta appeared to have intended. Helen was the more determined to overcome the obstacles that had been unfairly placed in her way, although how this could be achieved was less clear.

* * *

Steam ascended from the water, once thought to be the preserve of the goddess. Helen gazed at the accumulation of ages. The assembly rooms where Jane Austen had disported herself, above the baths of Tudor times, which in turn rested on the stones of Roman Aqueae Sulis. At home, there was the house, the monastery and under that the villa, once also the precinct of a god.

She checked her watch. Time to be going round to Dark Star. She left the baths and made her way through narrow lanes thronged with tourists and shoppers. She was really nervous this time. She knew she was running out of road. To make matters worse, Vernon Durbridge, the owner and operator of Dark Star, known as 'Do Bad' to his friends, and worse than that to the more numerous others, was widely reported to be an exceptionally unpleasant man.

She had a moment of panic when she couldn't find the address she had been given, then realised it was what looked like the door of a private house sandwiched between two shops. She buzzed the door bell and waited. Nothing. Should she try to phone? She waited a bit longer, then buzzed again. This time a disagreeable and incoherent sound emerged from the device, followed by a click as the door opened. She went in and climbed a narrow and uneven staircase. Reaching a small landing, she looked around for further directions, panicky again at the thought of not locating Durbridge. Behind one door she could hear someone talking intermittently. She knocked on the door, but got no reply. After another pause, she eased the door open cautiously. There was no reception area, and she simply found herself in a long room with a bare polished wooden floor. Along one side, three sash-windows were wide open. It was a warm, sunny day and a babble of French, Swedish and Japanese drifted in from the narrow, busy lane below.

She saw a tallish man of about forty with long, rather unkempt hair sitting with his back to her. Presumably that was Durbridge. He took no notice of her as she entered, not even looking up. In front of him was a bank of screens, holographic projectors and other devices. His attention constantly shifted from one piece of equipment to another, and occasionally he would speak into some part of the complex. As he continued to take no notice of her, she looked around the room. The only other furniture comprised two uncomfortable-looking upright wooden chairs. She took one of these, drew it fairly close to where Durbridge was sitting, sat down and waited for him. He showed no sign of being interested in her presence, but continued in frenzied engagement with his machines. Part angry, part anxious, she wondered if this was some sort of ad hoc personality test, perhaps to measure her powers of self-assertion. Eventually she shifted her position, crossed her legs and then said,

'I could come back later, if that's more convenient.'

He glanced sideways at her for a moment and then said, 'Great legs.'

What a pig she thought, but remained silent. Telling him off wouldn't be a great start to a vital interview. Instead she shifted slightly on her chair and pulled ineffectually at her skirt.

Durbridge assumed a mocking smile and said, 'Well, you needn't look so disapproving. You did yourself up like that knowing full well that I have a reputation for attractive girl friends. But alas, your efforts are wasted. If I had a business that operated from a big open plan office, I would tell some posh university to copy me a couple of dozen like you. But sadly I don't.'

She never seemed to get this one right, when interviewers were suspected to be male. Whether to wear the serious looking business outfit, or to flaunt whatever she'd got, or some compromise between the two. At the 'Cybertiser' she'd worn the serious outfit. That interview had seemed to go so well, she really felt she had it in the bag. Now she was certain the job must have gone to that girl she had seen waiting in reception done up like a hooker. Durbridge returned to his frenzied use of his machines, and took no further notice of her for a bit, but eventually without looking at her he said

'So can you dish the dirt on the local development mafia and the planning apparatchiks.'

'Er . . .'

'Well, I know who you are. You can't think I'm that out of touch. You're Nigel Roberts' daughter, aren't you? Why do you think I agreed to see you?'

What a shit. Had she done all she'd done to only be valued as her father's daughter.

'I've done . . .'

'You've done your nice little masters, which is no use to anyone on planet Reality.'

'It's considered one of the best courses.'

'Yes, you're a Clayton Clone. No doubt, you've been spanked for using semi colons or not using semi colons or whatever it is. Greta has a good eye for the trivial. I'll give her that. You clones can all fill up the page nice and neatly, but you've been castrated so that you never say anything of the slightest interest because it might offend someone.'

'I don't think I've been castrated at all. If you must know, I don't think Greta's much good. I'd say she was trivial, superficial and not very intelligent, not very appreciative of intelligent writing.'

A sour smile played at the corner of Durbridge's mouth before he said,

'I'd take you without your balls if you could give me some of the inside track on the development world in this part.'

She wondered if she should bluff it. The fact was she knew very little about her father's business. It had never been something that interested her or her mother, and had seldom been discussed at home. But there really wasn't much point in bluffing. Someone like Durbridge would work it out in a matter of days.

'I'm afraid I don't know much about my father's business.'

'I see. Over education has made you too posh for something grubby like the property market. Then I'm afraid it's good bye to you and your Grade 'A' legs.' He paused for a moment, and then added 'that's unless you've got the inside dirt on something else, which I doubt.'

For a moment her mind was blank with the sense of imminent failure, and then the chance of one last gamble presented itself.

'I might have something,' she said.

'Really?'

Clearly he didn't think there was much chance of that being the case, but then she told him something about the villa. For the first time, he stopped looking at screens, holo-casts and pieces of equipment, and gave her his full attention.

'Now that actually could be interesting. The punters like history and archaeology, and they like the idea that they haven't been getting the whole story, and that you're going to give it to them. There's a religious angle?'

'Is that a problem?'

'Not necessarily. Religion's not devoid of interest, although it be not true.'

'This involves some rather unorthodox religion.'

'Good. Behind the bland face of official religion lie esoteric secrets.'

'So it seems.'

'All right, I'll give you a try, and if it works you can make other contributions, preferably in the same area. You can fuck off now, but let me have something good.'

* * *

Getting back to the excavation, she found quite a crowd round the site office. She was frustrated to discover that she had missed one of the most exciting days of the entire project. With parts of the site already being filled in, as the end of the work approached, a quick exploratory trench across some of the drains of the lower church had uncovered a hoard of silver objects. She had arrived just in time to see this new discovery. A security van waited outside to take the find to safe keeping at the museum.

Helen went into the site office. Lizzie was standing next to James. There was something about her body language that suggested more than just an interest in what James was telling her. She was an attractive girl. No doubt she wouldn't have much difficulty in getting James into bed if the opportunity offered. Helen started to examine the silver objects spread out on the site office table. She felt a sudden sadness as she looked at this remnant of a lost religion and culture.

'It's unusual to find a hoard like this on a villa site,' James said. 'It's normally somewhere remote that robbers wouldn't think to look.'

'In my dreams, I knew we'd left something behind.'

James frowned at this, and said,

'A lot of this silver could be interpreted as Gnostic. Proscribed Christianity. Found in Britain in association with some forms of paganism. Look at this dish.'

He pointed out the largest object of the collection. The dish was more like a huge silver disk with human and satyr dancers circling the entire surface. There were a number of other plainer silver dishes and vessels and then a large quantity of small silver spoons. James indicated the spoons and said,

'They're a mixture. Some have symbols of cults we've found elsewhere in Britain. Faunus or Nodens, where the spoons are associated with intoxicants for heightened awareness, others are Christian with the chi-rho.'

He pointed out a number of the elegant little spoons and then one that shocked her. It was inscribed to Censorina.

'Something else has turned up in those drains,' James said. 'Come and see for yourself.'

He led her out and round to the back of the site office. She saw a battered round lead water trough or tank of some kind, perhaps half a metre deep and a metre or so across.

'What is it? Is it important or something?' She said.

'What they always refer to as a lead tank. There've been a couple of dozen found in Roman Britain, but none in the rest of the Empire. Definitely Christian. Look you can see the chi-rho down there. And the alpha and omega, but the omega is first, death before birth. They always seem to be connected to baptismal sites. Suggests a rite only practised in Britain.

'Unconventional practises that the Saxons were hired to stamp out. This is something important, James. Don't let the bastards make you airbrush this out. You promise you'll stand up to them.'

'Let's not have this argument again. You know I'm limited in what I can do.'

'You limit yourself. You've got to be stronger. Learn to break out, take risks.'

*   *   *

The find of ancient treasure at the villa was national news. She watched it unfold on the screen in her work room. There was a painstaking visual presentation, but the commentary annoyed her, saying mainly that the large hoard of silver indicated the wealth of this Roman agricultural centre. After this she had a message from Durbridge:-

> 'You're in luck. Your villa's what people want to hear more about. Debunk what the TV was saying, and put a controversial spin on the whole thing. The punters will lap that up.'

Next day the site closed. She walked down past it to the village already nostalgic for the summer she had spent there.

She looked forward to visiting James next week. Would that be prelude to living together? She wasn't sure. It felt a bit premature, but on the other hand she felt a bit foolish living at home at her age.

The only problem in writing her piece was that James had all along stressed that he had to adopt a low profile with his theory of the Saxon conquest, and especially anything referring to a lost religion. But she was angry with all this hiding and lying. She remembered how disgusted she had been with all of them that time at the museum, and the chance to show up the TV commentary looked too good to miss.

Besides holding back would make her story less interesting, and after all this was her one chance to establish herself in her chosen career. Several times she deleted sections that might embarrass James, only to put them back when she realised that her story had lost some of its previous sting. In the end she held nothing back.

*   *   *

James had drunk rather too much with friends the night before. He got the call to Professor Archibald's office just as he was thinking he needed another cup of coffee. Archibald's ample form overflowed his chair and his jowls trembled slightly as he announced the bad news. He showed him Helen's piece in Dark Star, then much worse the way that in a matter of hours the popular media had picked up the theme of suppressed information. Beyond that feedback was already coming in from a noisy fringe that spoke confidently of ley lines leading through the villa to Stonehenge.

'The ministry were on the phone this morning. They're furious. This woman, Helen Roberts, I'd heard about her already. She was your summer shag on the site.'

As he said this he rocked back slightly on his chair, and his jowls trembled again, James suspected he was indulging some fantasy of discarded underwear and hot, young limbs.

'We were in a relationship.'

'As I said, she was your summer shag. And this media disaster we've got is the result of your highly indiscrete pillow talk.'

'I'd no idea . . .'

All he could really focus on was his anger at Helen and his feeling of betrayal. Trying to undo the damage she'd done was beyond him at the moment.

'You'd no idea. Very true. Now I have to tell you the consequences of your idea or rather lack of idea. Actually, the ministry wanted us to get rid of you forthwith. It's fortunate for you that your type of contract makes that quite inconvenient. A tribunal, a court case even, that could throw up more of this Helen Roberts' crap. So I suppose I'd better tell you where we're going from here. This morning as quickly as possible, you will draft an authoritative denunciation of the Helen Roberts' piece.'

'I think some of it's true.'

Archibald's large face seemed to swell further and his eyes to bulge at this,

'For God's sake, who's interested in truth, this is about our jobs and our budget. Truth! Who do you think you are? Jesus Christ, or the Buddha or someone.' He paused for a moment and then continued, 'Following on that there'll be important changes to the department. We've agreed to cease coverage of this post-Roman period as such. I offered that to them as a sop, and it soothed them down a bit.'

'But that's period. It's badly misunderstood. My aim's to set that right.'

'Correction, it was your period. Or rather it wasn't your period. Your period never existed as anything viable. Did you ever read '1984'? Your period's this piece of paper, and now it disappears into the carbon-friendly rubbish chute just here by my desk. As for misunderstanding, it's you that have badly misunderstood the purpose of this department. Surely you're old enough to have outgrown student ideas about interest and purpose. This department is a machine to churn out investment bankers or hairdressers, or whatever the government thinks we need to get through our various problems. It's also a machine for paying my salary and yours, although you don't seem to deserve yours. Who cares about true or false? Certainly not our paymasters. Who cares about the Saxon conquest? They won, That's all that matters.'

'So what am I supposed to work on now?'

'You can assist me with the study of Byzantine trade routes in Britain. Byzantium was the only decent civilisation on this side of the world in your period, so why not be sensible and study that.'

Just for a moment in his mind's eye James saw the Byzantine galleys rise and fall on the blue swell as they lay at anchor at Tintagel. Further out galleys departed, turning south towards the eastern Med. Trade routes? Did those stop here or run further up towards the north? Perhaps some of those galleys did turn the other way towards the north. Perhaps evidence for his theory lay there too.'

Later when he had extricated himself from Archibald's office, he sent a message to Helen.

'You have completely betrayed me. Your piece has destroyed everything I had done in my career so far. You sold me to Dark Star. How much did they pay? Is thirty pieces of silver still the going rate? We're over. It's finished.'

She came back within minutes.

'I realise I've made a terrible mistake. I'm terribly sorry. Can we meet up and talk about it?'

He replied without hesitation,

'No. How can I respect someone who shows such a callous disregard for others. You've just used me. — Please, never try to contact me again.'

He regretted the awful finality of that message almost as soon as he had sent it. He considered several times sending something that mitigated his sentence, but each time his anger and disappointment with her stopped him. But if he had seen her crying, he would soon have weakened.

Chapter 11

Vendetta

Ten past nine in the morning. The pullman bus drivers on strike. Branwen was crammed in with other commuters on the new Whitehall line. In the summer heat, the air conditioning had failed, as it often did on the newer lines. Escaping from the commuter hell, she hurried to her office. Ministry for Culture, Entertainment and Country Crafts, it proclaimed at the entrance, but she noted to herself that even a faint interest in any of these areas was a career negative here. How long before she could move on to something with more life in it. This one was just a port in a storm. She must give her head hunter another prod. Her desk's morning meeting was already in progress. As she came in, Christine, her head of department was saying,

'I want you all to think hard on damage limitation measures for this Roman villa affair. We need to get the media to label this stuff as fringe.'

Seeing Branwen slip into a vacant seat, she continued, 'We like to start our meeting on time, at sharp on 8.30.'

'Thanks, I've been fucking scouring the hypernet most of the night. And I'd still be on time, if it wasn't for the criminal transport system in this city.'

'Has your night shift been productive?'

'Yes, as a matter of fact, it has. I know how we can stifle this Helen Roberts woman. We can gag this Dark Star blog.'

'That might not be so easy,' Christine said.

'We can if we have our wits about us, and I leave the answer to that question open. I've found out a lot of stuff about this Vernon Durbridge runs it. His revenue comes from the ads, and wait for it, the ministry provides about a fifth of the ads. He's big with people in education and culture.'

'Even assuming we can simply cut off that revenue stream, will that be enough? His costs can't be that high,' Christine said.

'That's where my holonet nosing comes in. Durbridge has a big life style to support. A house in the Royal Crescent in Bath, a villa somewhere south, a taste for driving petrol-head cars in the carbon premium lane, and now that tart . . .'

'Tart?'

'Wife, I think she's called now. She used to be with that footballer. The one that was in that fight in Argentina.'

'So?'

'High maintenance. Say no more. The fact is he's living up to the hilt or probably beyond it. He shouldn't be able to take that sort of drop in income. Our terms should be that he dumps the Roberts girl, and any mention of this miserable excavation.'

Christine seemed to be searching for, but failing to find objections, before saying,

'Right then, we'll see if we can discretely apply some pressure on this Durbridge.'

'You could say you were grateful to me for saving the department's skin,' Branwen said.

'The decision results from the consensus of the meeting. Naturally, we note your contribution.'

'There's another thing you might note for the future. We've got a handle on the old fart that runs the museum, Sir Twit or whatever he's called. The love of his life is his premium vineyard, and that's generously supported by our Country Craft's section.'

'Also noted,' Christine said, 'and unless anybody's got something to add that concludes the meeting.'

Fat chance that anybody was going to add anything, Branwen thought. A line of disinterested attendees filed out. They mainly comprised two categories of young or youngish people. First were the pale faced young, who had over indulged on clubbing or drinking. Next were the slightly less young, who had been kept awake by children. None of them would have thought to search the holonet overnight. By the time they were getting enough sleep to actually think during the day, they would be considered too old for a cutting edge job, and would be promoted to strategy whatever that meant. Branwen followed them into their cramped and gloomy office space.

*   *   *

Once they had all gone, Christine took Brian, her number two, aside. 'How much longer have I got to put up with that woman?' she said.

'She's quite effective.'

'Who wants effective? It's all public, so I can't ignore her idea, but it means I'm going to have a turf war with Rupert. He just hates anybody interfering in how he allocates our advertising. Look, I want you to try and gather the necessary evidence so that we can fire her fairly cheaply and without too much fuss. Can you promise to do that?'

*   *   *

Nigel glanced at his watch as he hurried under the portico of the museum. Just like Sir Trevor to refuse to use the holophone. It wasn't as if he hadn't got staff to make the thing work for him. It was just his mindless conservatism. Coffee and biscuits were ready on the table when Nigel reached the meeting room. Sir Trevor reclined in a large leather chair, and apologised for not rising to greet Nigel, on account of his age and joints.

'Helen seems such a charming girl. I suppose you and Maria blame yourselves,' Sir Trevor said as soon as Nigel had seated himself.

'Blame ourselves, why should we . . .'

'Blame yourselves that such a good looking girl's turned out for the bad.'

'It's news to me that she's turned out for the bad.'

'This essay or thing she wrote. I don't understand a word of it, dear boy. That's how I was brought up. Leadership, not pouring over details. But it's made a lot of people angry. We've had some ministry busy bodies on the phone. Can't understand them, but they're not happy bunnies. And we've had the strangest people calling wanting to examine our reserve collection. One young woman thought the museum was on some sort of ley line.'

'If Helen made any mistake it was to speak her mind, and put down what she rightly or wrongly conceived to be the truth. What is sad is that it seems to have created a rift with her archaeological friend. I wasn't greatly taken with him, but I've never seen her so upset about anything.'

'I'm afraid I do blame you and Maria. You're too nice. Helen should have been curbed more. She was always a bit loud and outspoken for a young woman. And that progressive school . . .'

'There was nothing unusual about her school, except that it had high academic standards.'

'It seems that she must have mixed with a rather low type of boy, and they probably had the same sort at that university of hers. I didn't go to university myself. I've never seen the point of universities, especially for girls. A bad influence. She laughs at the sort of thing that we used to laugh at when we were young men. A properly brought up young woman doesn't do that. I'm afraid, Nigel, the fact is that she was badly brought up, badly brought up.'

'Have you brought me all the way here to complain about Helen's upbringing.'

Sir Trevor looked uneasy at this, and cast around the room as if looking for some of his staff, but clearly he had decided to keep this meeting private.

'The trustees,' Sir Trevor said, and then didn't seem to know how to finish. Nigel knew that the word 'trustees' meant something Sir Trevor had decided on by himself, or possibly with the help of one or two of his yes-man staff.

'My friend at the palace phoned. Princess Mary's been cancelled,' Sir Trevor said finally.

'What! They're pulling out just because of this little piece on the holonet.' At a stroke Nigel saw the scenario of himself on the podium in front of the museum with the princess, and then escorting her through the new galleries vapourise, but he recovered himself and said,

'Well, too bad. Who can we get to replace her?'

'The trustees,' Sir Trevor resumed, 'have decided that in view of the bad publicity surrounding the villa, the reputation of the whole museum might suffer from having it prominently displayed. We have returned to the idea of mounting the Cloppard collection.'

'That's outrageous . . .'

'I don't think it's your place to talk like that.'

'Don't you? This museum is the most important collection of Roman material in the country. The new silver discovery at the villa is almost without rival. It's totally against the spirit of your articles of association . . .'

'The trustees . . .'

'Fuck the trustees. They're just so many cardboard cut outs. Your friends and acquaintances. They have absolutely no relevant experience and not even much interest in the antiquities.'

'I have complete confidence in the trustees. The most solid people.'

'Solid in the head, I should say. Was the decision unanimous?'

'Well ... er ... the decisions of the trustees are confidential, old boy.'

That meant it wasn't unanimous, and Nigel knew the one trustee, a younger man called Adrian, now seemingly prospering in the slave mines of the City, who might at a pinch have an independent view. He got up, saying as he did so,

'That was a bad decision, and you're going to find that you regret it.'

Sir Trevor leant back in his chair, and stared at Nigel in such an uncomprehending way that Nigel became worried that he was on the verge of some form of cardiac event. He muttered a good bye, but on the way out he whispered a warning to Miss Bell, the PA, that she should keep an eye on the old man.

Going back through the museum, he wondered what action he should take. People didn't trifle with him. They didn't make promises, and then back out for no good reason. Sir Trevor was going to regret his attempt to take the line of least resistance. By the time Nigel was back at the entrance, he had a plan of action. He phoned Adrian, and arranged to meet him for a drink after work, near his office in the City.

From there Nigel went to the high speed. Arriving in London, he was irritated to discover the pullman buses were on strike, making his five-year discount offer card for the service unusable. He'd only invested in this extravagance because of Maria's phobia with the tube, and now he was being denied the little bit of benefit he might have enjoyed. Instead, he boarded an ancient and very hot train, and had to stand the whole way as it creaked its way through tunnels and cuttings to the eastern edge of the City. Emerging from this, he could see Adrian's office building, the so-called

Copper Spike, towering 600 metres into the summer haze. He had to wait for twenty minutes in the reception area amidst a tropical profusion of pot plants. He quite enjoyed the scene of purposeful comings and goings that contrasted with the more languid atmosphere of the Cotswolds and the Marches.

Eventually, Adrian appeared to greet him. He had seemed quite a young man when Nigel had last seen him, but in the meantime he had grown rather portly and his hair had thinned a bit, taking him over the tipping point from youth into early middle age. Adrian steered him into a narrow side turning, and then down steps into a dark underground place, where the owners seemed intent on expensively recreating the poverty that might have existed in such a back street in the nineteenth century. They bought a bad, but stunningly expensive, bottle of wine. Nigel took a draught of the sour liquid, and decided to move quickly to the point.

'I was glad you could see me this evening. There's something I wanted to discuss about the museum.'

'The museum?' Adrian looked a bit vague.

'You are a trustee, aren't you?'

'Oh, ah, yes, the Prima Britannia Museum, you mean.'

'Yes, I think you weren't so happy about a decision on the collection to go into the new wing.'

'Collection?'

'The Cloppard collection. Animal pictures.'

'Oh, um, yes, pictures of cows and pigs and things. No one would want to look at stuff like that.'

'Look,' Nigel said, 'for various reasons I won't go into, I have sponsored a display of Roman material for the new wing. The Cloppard seems to be supplanting that. I want your support for the Roman material.

'No can do,' Adrian replied. 'I did argue a bit for your Roman things, but the rest of them are scared of trouble. Something about what some young girl wrote on the holonet, and next thing there was a jobsworth bureaucrat on the phone giving Sir T. an earful.'

'I think you'll find it's not as straightforward as just a four-to-one vote. I did some homework while I was on the high-speed. Charitable Governance Act (2044). Under that, one trustee plus three or more outside people can demand a judicial review of any major decision of a charitable body that appears to involve a material investment not related to the original purpose of that body.'

Adrian's small piggy face had taken on a worried expression. It was clear to Nigel that Adrian had not expected there to be any purpose to this drink other than to provide Nigel with some company during a spare hour or two in the City.

'Hm, I don't know that I'm in much of a position to tackle something like that. Look, Sir T's a raving snob. He only asked me on board because my Dad's a Right Hon. for some reason. I haven't got much time to spend on the museum. I'm working all hours. I can't afford to get fired or even miss a bonus at the moment. Celia mortgaged us up to the hilt to get the place she wanted. High-interest loan from Schlacher Sisters Private Banking. They're very quick to repossess if there's any hint of a drought of cash.'

'Perhaps you could help me if I do you a little favour.'

'Favour?' A gleam had come into Adrian's piggy eyes.

'You know the Delphinium Centre.'

'The place those Friends of the Twentieth Century created about?'

Nigel frowned. It annoyed him that the ridiculous complaints of the friends had managed to reach even the ears of someone like Adrian, high in his gleaming copper tower.

'Forget the friends,' Nigel said. 'The Delphinium's been a runaway commercial success. Now we're raising money to extend it. We're taking our company public. Our advisors think it's going to be a really good one. I can get you into the initial placing. You should be able to take a nice turn on that.'

'That's very generous of you indeed,' Adrian said with every sign of enthusiasm. 'Right on. I'm with you and the Romans.'

* * *

When Nigel got home he was surprised to find Helen lying listless on the sofa, and listening to an animal programme. Normally, she was either out with friends or hard at work on some project.

'You look a bit down,' he said.

'Yes, Dark Star isn't going to use me anymore. I really can't understand it. I know the piece about the villa was a real hit. I suppose it was something mysterious about my style. Did it lack flair?'

'Rubbish. It reads very well. Dark Star has been leant on. That's as clear as anything. Believe me, there's a lot going on behind the scenes with this.'

He paused and then a thought came to him.

'I've got an idea for you. You've made a minor splash on the holonet already. The museum is planning to use the Cloppard rubbish instead of the Roman stuff. I want you to campaign against that.'

Helen turned the television off just as a huge carnivore smashed into the neck of an luckless herbivore. 'I know the person we need,' she said.

'Who?'

'Hermione. She did fine art, and now she's at some gallery in Bond St. She should be able to give me the right talk the talk words to leave those Cloppard animals dead in the water.'

* * *

Hermione called back on the holophone only a couple of days after getting Helen's enquiry about the Cloppard. Seeing her after a long gap in time, Helen felt uncomfortable with the fact that she found herself still living a student-type life. Hermione had become a young business woman discarding the short hair, jeans and odd bits of sports clothes of her student years for a neat pony tail and an elegant black dress.

Hermione told her what to say to ensure the comprehensive slaughter of the Cloppard animals, and then with some glee added,

'And I dug some extra dirt you might use. The main artist was a Henry Luggershall. In fact, artist is a bit of an exaggeration. He started life as a butcher's assistant in Gloucester. He obtained just enough skill in drawing to enable him to copy the shapes of animals drawn by other artists, then fill in the space with some of the dingy paint that you mention. And there's a final stage to the story — a bit sad, really. His artistic career may have petered out. At any rate, the records of the Gloucester Assizes show that five years later he was hanged for stealing a sheep, a real one, not a painted one.'

'Poor man. But could the paintings still be valuable, or have some sort of nerdy historic interest.'

'Not valuable certainly. There's too much of that sort of thing around. Of course there's some limited historic interest, just the fact that people wanted that sort of painting is interesting, but for a major museum like the Prima that hardly justifies displaying more than one or two examples.'

*   *   *

They sat glumly opposite one another in the same meeting room as previously. Sir Trevor and his assistant Miss Bell on one side of the table, Nigel, his lawyer, Harold, and Adrian on the other side. Sir Trevor looked at Nigel with a watery eye,

'I can't understand the necessity for this meeting. Surely, it's quite straight forward. The trustees have decided to mount the Cloppard Collection. That all there is to it, old boy.'

'We contest that right,' Nigel said

'Who exactly are we,' Miss Bell asked.

'Adrian here as one of the trustees, myself and Maria and Helen as interested non-trustees.'

'I understand that Maria and Helen are both minors in which case their objection is legally void.' Miss Bell said.

'Maria is my wife.'

'Am I to understand that your wife is not a minor?'

'She is not.'

'But Helen is only sixteen,' Sir Trevor said.

'It is not certain that the objections of minors are always invalid,' Harold said. 'In the case Bufton v. Bognor Regis Leisure Facilities it was held that if . . .'

'Stop,' Nigel said. 'This is all totally irrelevant. Helen is twenty-five years old.'

'Are you sure,' Sir Trevor said. 'I felt certain she was only sixteen.'

'Of course, I'm sure. I know how old my own daughter is.'

'I can never remember how old mine are,' Sir Trevor said.

Miss Bell stared down at the table. Adrian was looking out of the window at the grey sky, with an expression that conveyed a mixture of boredom and despair, while Harold thumbed through his massive bundle of documents. Eventually, Miss Bell spoke,

'The material point is why one trustee and three people unrelated to the museum should object, even if they are technically a quorum under the Charitable Governance Act.'

'My client relies on, amongst other cases, the ruling in Marvins v. Brayside Galleries. The gallery was established in Edwardian times to commemorate the fact that the area had been patronised by a number of minor pre-Raphaelite artists.

109

Amongst those who used to stay there in those summers were . . .'

'Harold, I don't think we need to go into every one of the artists. Just the matter of the dispute over the use of the gallery,' Nigel said.

'Ah, that brings us forward to the middle part of this century. The chairman of Brayside at the time was one Edward Pooks-Smith. Pooks-Smith had had a distinguished career as a chartered surveyor in Hong Kong, becoming a partner in — Oh, but I suppose you don't need to know all that. In his retirement, the said Pooks-Smith had taken to painting water colours of the area. It's still a very unspoilt part even today. It also happened that some new space had been added to the gallery just before Pooks-Smith became chairman. He decided with the support of the majority of trustees, who happened to be his golfing partners, to fill the extension to the gallery with his own paintings. However two trustees and several local people with an interest in the arts objected. A review of the governance of the gallery concluded that the Pooks-Smith paintings were of no artistic merit, and could not lawfully be displayed in the gallery.'

'You can't say the Cloppard has no artistic value,' Sir Trevor said. 'I've always been told that it's very highly regarded.'

'Our expert opinion is that it's artistically worthless,' Nigel said.

He was only basing this on Hermione's informal opinion, but that would do for the time being. 'Apparently, the author wasn't really a proper artist. Just a copyist of other artists, who, incidentally, ended badly. He was hanged for stealing a sheep.'

'Serves the young devil right,' Sir Trevor said. 'These artistic types often go to the bad. Still even if the Cloppard doesn't suit arty types, it's still a time capsule.'

'There's so many similar things that even there the value's limited. It would never justify filling a good part of a major museum.'

'I can't believe I'm being treated like this, after all the years of work I've devoted to this museum,' Sir Trevor said.

Miss Bell pushed aside some papers that were in front of her on the table and said,

'It is possible there is some scope for compromise between our positions.'

'I don't see any requirement for my client to make concessions to you given the untenable nature of your position,' Harold said.

'Litigation is never good news for anyone, except you lawyers,' Miss Bell replied.

'What are you going to suggest,' Nigel said.

'That the villa material occupies the main area of the new wing. However, some of the less notable mosaics and the in my opinion rather uninteresting photos of the villa site that were to be displayed on the staircases and in the enlarged cafeteria should be replaced by parts of the Cloppard.'

'For my part, I'd rather see the whole of the Cloppard dumped. I've never seen such rubbish,' Adrian said.

'I am afraid I've realised that you don't have much appreciation of any of these matters,' Sir Trevor said. 'Strange when your father is a man of such taste and discrimination. I seem to have been sadly mistaken in recommending you to the other trustees.'

'We do seem to be on a convergence path,' Nigel said. 'Miss Bell, would you send me a detailed draft of what you propose.'

'I'm less than happy with this,' Sir Trevor said. 'I don't like the approach that any of you are taking.'

Miss Bell gave Sir Trevor a glance which seemed to say "I'll be able to twist the old bastard's arm."

'The other matter we should look at is the opening ceremony for the new wing,' Nigel said. 'What's the chance that the palace will relent, and let us have Princess Mary?'

'Helen's unfortunate outbursts on the holonet have ruined my standing at the palace,' Sir Trevor said.

'We can't even get Prince Edmund let alone Princess Mary.' Miss Bell said. 'Sir Trevor's friend at the palace tells us everything to do with this museum and the Roman villa is out-of-bounds for the whole of the royal flock. The best we've been able to do is the Duchess of Kilmarnock.'

'But Kilmarnock is just one of Babington's spare parts,' Adrian said.

'Kilmarnock's all we can get,' Miss Bell said, 'unless you want some floosie from a soap opera, and Sir Trevor doesn't think that's very appropriate.'

Nigel recalled that when this Babington had been prime minister seemingly his only achievement had been that when faced with the dual complaints of a shortage of highly-placed people to dignify events, and that those who did so were disproportionately male, he had tried to kill two birds with one stone by creating twelve life-Duchesses.

For her part the now-Duchess of Kilmarnock had been a senior politician until it was decided she should take the blame for the purchase of a more than usually expensive and ineffective missile. She received her elevation to the rank of Duchess in exchange for the understanding that she would spend the rest of her mortal span shaking hands with local worthies. The name, Duchess of Kilmarnock, sounded to Nigel like one of those big steam locomotives from the last century. He had had a book of pictures of them at home when he was a child. He envisaged a black and white picture with some such caption as 'Duchess of Kilmarnock hauls the 4.28pm. Preston to Carlisle express on the incline out of Carnforth Junction, July 13th 1956.

*   *   *

It was raining heavily. Some bunting hung limply on the front of the museum, and the square in front was almost deserted. There was some difficulty in finding Nigel's name on the list of invitees. The reception was of modest size, filling less than half the grand entrance hall. Sir Trevor and Miss Bell were guiding the Duchess through the guests. She had a listless, disinterested expression, possibly still turning over in her mind how she came to be blamed for the dud missile purchase.

Nigel overheard Sir Trevor introducing a man from Nigel's own village as "one of the donors that I told you about", and then pass on without appearing to notice Nigel. He circled round and came up in front of the Duchess, just as Sir Trevor was about to introduce her to a local councillor. Nigel stepped quickly in front of the councillor, seized the Duchess's limp hand, and introduced himself as the sponsor of the new galleries.

'Mr Roberts was at school with my son,' Sir Trevor said, as if to excuse an intrusion.

The Duchess had already ducked away, a well-honed skill that had no doubt helped her along the road towards responsibility for weapons of mass destruction. Sir Trevor moved on without further comment, while Nigel was rewarded with an icy stare from Miss Bell.

The time came for the official opening speeches, and Nigel found himself squeezed into the last but one row at the back. The Duchess did not seem too well apprised of the main purpose of the new wing, dwelling mainly on the historic interest of the Cloppard collection, and coming up with the dubious claim that the artist had been hanged as a radical agitator in the area. She rounded off with congratulations to Sir Trevor for recently obtaining a fine collection of Roman silver, with no mention of its connection to the villa. Finally she named a number of donors amongst whom Nigel's name was not included. The Duchess's contribution was followed by a speech from Lady Cloppard, in which she gave a rambling account of her family's involvement in the local area, and complained about the lack of space for a proper display of the collection.

After this there was a tour of the new wing. The Duchess, Sir Trevor, Lady Cloppard and Miss Bell had a small privileged group round them, while the other guests made their own way round. On entering the new wing, Nigel immediately noticed that the plaque commemorating his contribution was much smaller than agreed, and had been placed too high up to be easily seen. That at least could and would be dealt with by lawyers.

Already brimming with resentment, he saw more scope for litigation in the actual displays. Although most of the items were there, the interpretation of the underground areas left their function unclear, which was not in accord with the fine print of his agreement with the museum. Similarly, the Roman silver was well displayed, but as in the Duchess's speech, there was no reference to its connection to the villa, again not in accord with the agreement. The cafeteria had been made over for a formal lunch, but on attempting to gain entry to this, he was informed that he only had a white card, and would find sandwiches and a cash bar in the main entrance hall.

He left the museum angrily only to find that his new car, one of the much praised 'Eco Heroine Series 8' range had disappeared from its reserved parking space. Phoning to report a theft, an automated reply system informed him that for security reasons that vehicle had been removed and destroyed in a controlled explosion. Nigel wondered who would bother to try to assassinate the Duchess, but then he realised that the security had probably been originally put in place for Princess Mary's visit.

The rain continued to soak down reducing his expensive suit to a soggy mess as he walked through the centre of the town. He considered a line of taxis, but thought that he hadn't got where he was through extravagance. He just made the afternoon bus to Northcombe, only because it had been held up by security diversions. On the bus, sitting next to a woman from his village, he was regaled with a catalogue of complaints about the disruption caused by the museum event. This included the remark that the Duchess only got this attention because she had always been rich and lived in a big house. In reality, the Duchess had grown up on a tough estate, and had been one of the very few to ever make the leap from her sink school to a good university, but it amused him to let his neighbour's misconception stand.

A light rain continued to fall as still consumed by anger, he walked up the lane from the village past the now silent and deserted villa site. He found himself wondering what resentful ghosts might lurk there. Arriving home, he sent a detailed account of the day's proceedings to Helen. No doubt, she would make some mileage with that on her holoblog. But that would not be enough. The museum project that had begun as a public relations ploy had become a vendetta, in which he was determined to show Sir Trevor and Miss Bell that he was not to be trifled with.

Chapter 12

Hindley Grange

They were going to pay for this. All their shit would hit the fan once her case came to court. What did they mean that she had thrown her phone at Brian. She had simply shown him her phone to make the dullard understand that she couldn't afford a decent phone after not getting a salary increase. As for calling the assistant head of human resources a fat-arsed dimwit that had been a set up. Getting a whole series of people to ask the same silly question, so that she didn't notice that the last one was someone important, was simply a dirty trick.

Anyway, she had seen this coming, the shits, and she had prepared something that might with a bit of luck do even more damage to them than the pending court case. It was so easy. Their systems were so unbelievably sloppy. It wasn't even a question of hacking. There was stuff going back to the nineteenth century in cardboard boxes in the basement. Apparently an attempt to bring the material online had failed because the IT department couldn't come to terms with physical size of the older documents. One had to sign stuff out, but no one ever asked for it back. So in her hand, she now had original documents that could at a pinch be twisted round to support James' barmy ideas.

It was really a question of who was the bigger bastard. Her erstwhile employers or that creep, James. She did resent him. He had smothered her with an eight-year sentence of petit-bourgeois domesticity, not to mention persistent conversations about the most obscure and uninteresting bit of this septic isle's history. And his ideas about history weren't just boring, they were downright annoying. They had to be wrong. Religion couldn't be that important. There had been wars and persecutions, but surely that was a just a mask for class or ethnic tensions or some bullshit of that kind.

She was a historian, and she'd seen enough of James' work to despise archaeology. Muddy people wittering on about post holes. Well, even that was only if they could drag their eyes away from the young volunteer bending over said post hole. Whatever it was, they had no grasp of the wider forces shaping history. But none of that mattered. James had these weird ideas, and she just might be able to put him into play, so as to give her former employers mega pain.

The next thing was how to get the documents to him. She mustn't leave an electronic trail. Safest would be to take the documents to him in person, but she did not want the tedious journey nor the face-to-face meeting. He did not merit that amount of trouble. Similarly, the cost of sending such bulky items with a private courier did not seem justified for something that might end up mainly benefiting James. Then she hit on the idea of sending them by post, that once proud but now nearly defunct service. She couldn't remember when she had last seen a post office, but looking on the holonet, she found one only a few hundred metres from her flat, albeit in a street whose name was unfamiliar. Walking over there, she found herself in a narrow grey road that she could not remember having been in before. The post office was not in what she regarded as a proper building, but was just a gap in a windowless wall. As she turned in the door, she was accosted by some kind of official in a shapeless blue uniform,

'Not here, you want the courier office, third on the left.'

She managed to brush him off, but moving further into the dim interior, she could understand why he had identified her as unsuitable for the place. A huge queue zig zagged to-and-fro across the whole area. Although she was wearing cheap, casual clothes, she felt like a fashion icon in this company. Everyone seemed either very old or on the verge of dereliction. The space they were in appeared well suited to the clientele. The floor made of some form of concrete was uneven and slicks of dirty water had formed in places. The walls were plastered with various incomprehensible notices in varying unpleasant shades of pink and beige. Above the counter a large illuminated sign proclaimed the title 'Royal Mail' except that the 'R' in 'Royal' flickered on and off.

Only one position was open, and most of the transactions took a long time, often involving a protracted argument, or the clerk making a phone call, or worse still leaving the counter, presumably to consult a superior. As she edged closer to the counter, she developed a growing hatred of the other customers. They never had anything that was straight forward. With some, every stage of the process was accompanied by a bombardment of questions. Sometimes they had actually moved away from the counter, but were suddenly inspired to leap back with a new question. Why do you bother, you old git. You're going to drop dead any moment, and you'll be better off when you do, Branwen thought. Several times she contemplated giving up, and going to the courier office, or even abandoning this long-shot project altogether. But a mixture of not wanting to write off the time she had already wasted, desire to save money and hatred of her employers kept her in her place in the queue.

At last her turn came. The clerk took a long time to weigh and stamp her package, frowning as he did so.

'Can I see your SSC,' he said eventually.

'What?'

He fixed a patronising gaze on her that made it clear that he thought she had some difficulties, and said very slowly and clearly,

'Your SSC, show it to me.'

'What is it? I don't think I have one.'

'Yes, you do.' And then speaking even more slowly, 'Your state subsidy card, one like this.' He held up a grubby white plastic card, and for good measure pointed to it.

'No, I don't have one.'

'It's your proof of low income.'

'I don't have a low income.'

This caused a baffled expression. He left his seat, and Branwen saw him talking to a middle-aged woman who kept looking at her. It reminded her of seeing the teachers talking about her at school, when some idiot claimed she had been misbehaving. Eventually, the woman came over and spoke to her,

'You have to pay the full price if you don't have an SSC. It would be cheaper to use a courier service.'

'How much would it be?'

The woman glanced at the package, and then named a price that would have bought a rather good bottle of wine.

'Oh, all right I'll pay that. I've spent so much time on this already.'

But this was not the end of her problems. When she produced her credit card, she was informed that the Royal Mail did not accept credit cards. She proffered a high-denomination bank note. This resulted in a search for the key to a drawer that contained the infrequently used supply of cash.

'Hurry up, we haven't got all day,' she heard from a large woman behind her.

Yes, you have, Branwen thought and what's more this is probably the most exciting bit of your dreary day.

Eventually, the drawer was opened, but was then found to contain not quite enough change.

'It doesn't matter, that'll be all right,' Branwen said.

But the clerk was determined to do things by the book. He left his desk and consulted with the middle-aged woman again, who found the key to another drawer. By this time more sounds of disapproval were emerging from the queue behind her. At last the clerk returned with her change, and she managed to make her escape.

'About time too,' the large woman said as she moved forward with an awkward shaped package that looked destined to create even greater problems.

As Branwen moved towards the door there was a loud peal of thunder, heralding another of the ever more frequent and violent summer storms. Nearing the door, she saw a virtual wall of rain. The entrance began to fill with soaked passers-by seeking refuge. The roadway was awash, and began to overlap the pavement in places, while at the same time a large puddle formed within the doorway of the post office.

The enforced stop, huddled amongst damp people, allowed her to contemplate the possible consequences of her action. Those could vary. James might ignore the documents, or fail in his attempt to make use of them. On the other hand, he might do something that would have unpredictable knock-on effects within the intellectually stagnant pool of academic archaeology and history. That she hoped might bring acute discomfort to her former employers.

*   *   *

James shifted uneasily on his seat. A meeting of the whole archaeological department. Something that never happened in the real life of virtual exchanges and snatched one-to-one conversations. James eyed his colleagues. George Cairn-Brown. The isotope man. The pride of the department. Four times runner up for the Heinrick-Trokig prize for isotope archaeology. He would really have got it the last time, but for a rival who demonstrated that the Saxon population of Canterbury were really Irish. It was the sort of three-card trick that isotope researchers loved to pull.

James glanced sideways at him. Somehow he was always expecting Cairn-Brown to say or write something interesting. The intellectual pinnacle on which he was placed in the university seemed to call for that. It just never actually happened. His papers were nothing more than tables of numbers riddled with decimal points. Cairn-Brown himself was out of it, as he always seemed to be — staring straight ahead through rimless glasses. And who wore glasses nowadays anyway, except the very old or the very young? Was it an affectation, the lingering idea that it was something that intellectuals wore, or was he just too removed from the stream of life to select something more convenient? Next to Cairn-Brown was Trish, her jaw thrust slightly forward, no doubt poised to make one of those cheery remarks that James always found slightly irritating.

Professor Archibald entered, head down, not looking at them.

'Sorry to keep you people waiting,' he said as he settled into his chair, shifted some papers round on his desk, and then glanced around at the other three.

'Yes, nice to get us all together,' he started. 'Hm, coming up to the beginning of the academic year. I think we need to talk a bit about the organisation of the department.'

There was a silence. James felt that whatever was coming would not be good news. The others seemed to have less sense of danger, Cairn-Brown staring blankly ahead, Trish still with her eager jaw line.

'The fact is we are facing a number of problems,' Archibald resumed. 'A certain amount of unfavourable comment with our last flagship excavation, falling student numbers, more rival courses.'

'We're still getting regional aid, aren't we,' Trish said. 'It's a depressed region. Everyone with get up and go has got up and gone.'

'I don't think that's a view calculated to make us very popular locally.'

'It's what they say themselves.'

James glanced at the cheap reproduction on the wall of the meeting room. An Elizabethan seaman pointed out to sea, and talked to two wondering youngsters. Another time, with a hope and independence long forgotten. Through the window, he could see the remnants of a giant supermarket and a holiday camp ineptly converted into the northernmost extension of their campus. Beyond he glimpsed the sullen grey of the sea. Iconic buildings might have brought their department to the attention of the brighter type of student, but the architectural committee had rejected six more imaginative designs for the existing mix of grey boxes and bad conversions. The models of the more promising designs were still gathering dust in the basement storage.

For a moment Archibald's usual pompous self-confidence seemed to deflate into weariness, but then he recovered himself, and said,

'Our paymasters don't have endless patience. We need to show some ability to attract archaeological students.'

'You can always fill up with foundationals. They do four years so that fills even more places.'

'An extra year on the course reworking their failed schooling. Costs money. They're getting wise to that ploy.'

'So you've some suggestions.'

Archibald frowned. It was pretty clear to James that he disliked the implication that this was any form of discussion between equals.

'I've decided on some changes to the department. I'm sorry James, but George is our most prestigious researcher and I've decided he should head up next year's flagship excavation. That may not be the most important thing from an academic point of view, more a bit of cheap showmanship, but they are the stuff that pull media coverage, and more important, that's what bears on student applications. James, of course you know we're not covering your post-Roman period any longer, because of the ministry, so someone else can have a go at our flagship work.'

To James' surprise the normally silent Cairn-Brown spoke first,

'I won't be able to spend more than four weeks on site. I've got a heavy load of work pencilled for next summer already.'

Before either James or Archibald could follow up, the authoritive presence of Archibald's PA was dominating the room.

'Excuse me, I've got the maintenance manager on the phone. There's a problem with cleaning the pigeon stuff from the roof of the atrium.'

'What sort of problem, there's never been a problem before.'

'No, it's the new regulations. The staff aren't allowed to reach upwards when they're on the top deck of the rig.'

'Well tell him it's got to be done this week. We've got the sixth form open day nearly on us. It's bad enough we haven't painted the place for six years.'

When this didn't seem to cut much ice with the PA, he continued, 'Haven't they got some things on poles that can get to it?'

'Storage say they don't have any record of ever having something like that.'

'Oh, that so ridiculous, so pathetic, tell them to bloody well try again.'

She retreated after this, although to James her expression suggested a smug assurance that nothing would be done about the pigeon excrement.

Archibald turned back to confront Cairn Brown and said,

'I don't think you've understood me properly. You're to move to excavation full time. James will take on our isotope research.'

Now James saw the plot. Archibald was determined to get him away from any excavation work that might lead to embarrassing findings, even at the price of damaging the department's one uncontroversial success in isotope work.

'The others don't know isotopes,' Cairn-Brown said. He took off the rimless glasses and glanced around the room with a surprised expression. It was the nearest he ever seemed to come to expressing emotion.

'You'll both get a fresh angle, and Trish you will move from rural settlement excavations to help James get to grips with isotopes.'

'No, I won't.' A grimness overtook her normally cheerful expression.

'It's not really for you to decide.'

'You can't demote, without a written warning on under performance. So far you haven't complained about my performance at all.'

'You're not being demoted. In fact, slightly promoted. Your scale will go up from 19b to 18c.'

'In the eyes of another employer an assistant position would be less impressive.'

'So you're thinking of leaving us.'

'No, but everyone has to look to the long term.'

'Human resources would back off from fighting at tribunal,' Cairn-Brown said. 'They're always afraid of getting to court. They can't get decent lawyers on our rates. They lost the last three cases, although they should have won them on any reasonable estimate.'

Archibald was looking dangerous. The bull surrounded by matadors. James could imagine him stomping the ground before charging.

'If you like, I'll swap with James,' Trish said, her cheerful countenance reappearing. We both need a change. I'll take on the villas, or the Byzantine harbours or whatever it is, and he can have a go at round houses and rural hutments.'

So that was her play, James thought. Jump from her hutment excavations to the high profile work on the back of the conflicts between the rest of them.

'I thought you said the hut circles and the round houses were more socially relevant. You said that's where 99% of the population lived and what life was like, while I was supposed to be excavating the 1% used by the rentier elite and the warlords. Have you changed your mind?'

'I wouldn't say that. We all need to broaden our experience. We could both benefit and George could concentrate on his isotopes.'

Archibald scowled and said, 'This wasn't intended to be a general debate. I had quite clear plans for the department . . .'

His PA was in the room again.

'It's the senior expenses committee. You're two minutes over time already. They're all waiting for you. Sir Clarke looks a bit impatient.'

'I hadn't really finished with this.'

She seemed to thrust out her ample chest, a gesture that seemed to happen whenever she encountered signs of defiance.

'They going to be discussing the wine purchases,' she said with the air of one delivering a masterstroke.

'Oh, yes, that's important, I need to be there.'

Archibald glanced at his recalcitrant staff, and said,

'All right, Trish, you can stick with your hut circles. But I'm swapping the other two of you between isotopes and flagship excavations, like it or not, you'll just have to work things out for yourselves.'

He gathered some papers from his desk and lunged off in the direction of the expenses meeting. James turned to the other two once they were outside in the corridor.

'Well, at least you saw Archibald off,' James said to Trish.

'He'll be looking to get his own back,' Cairn-Brown said and then to James. 'You'd better read my book on isotopes and origins.

'Yes, I will, and you'd better take a course on dealing with the media.'

Cairn-Brown looked at James as if he had lost his mind, turned, and walked off down the corridor.

Another big step down James thought. Isotopes were an important area, but it would take years to build a reputation in that, while he was diverted away from what he was actually interested in. If Archibald hadn't been called into the expenses meeting, he might have been tempted to go back in and resign. But no, there were strong arguments against the alternative. If he went to the 'Gate', he would be stepping out of the safe circle of academia, would become fringe and would never be allowed to return. On the other hand, his position here, with his unpopularity with Archibald, was becoming precarious.

*　　*　　*

Branwen had the unfamiliar feeling of being quietly pleased with her lot. She surveyed her new office with some satisfaction. It was quite spacious with an important looking desk, book cases and a side table and chairs where small meetings could be held. She overlooked a large square surrounded by squat, grey buildings forming the heart of the university campus. Students could be seen strolling to-and-fro or chatting in small groups.

Her exit from this university, some years ago, and well before she finally broke up with James, had been stormy, but her former boss had retired early, and she had returned not to her old department, but to the more important Department of Archaeology. Moreover, whereas she had been at the same level of seniority as James when she had left here, she was now his superior. In the intervening period, she had experienced redundancies and departures in anger, but each job had looked good on the CV, and each move had involved some measure of promotion. The last job at the ministry, miserable as it had been in practise, had made her look like a must-have for this university. So the end result of a turbulent process was that she was at a level that gave her some part in the management of James's efforts. She noted with amusement that James' own determined concentration on his work had not required that he receive any promotion.

Really her present post was just right for her purposes. Not much specific work load, but plenty of scope for interfering in other people's work and making trouble for anyone or anything that she disapproved of. Branwen decided it was time to pay James a visit. She strolled contentedly through the corridors of the university, and barged into his office without bothering to knock. Well, he didn't warrant that sort of politeness.

James was alone and head down over his computer. It was like the office she had had when last at this university, but a bit worse. It was really a cubby hole rather than an office with just enough room for his chair, a desk cluttered with equipment and papers and another chair for a visitor. Books and boxes were piled in corners and along any empty wall space. The one small window looked out over vans and lorries in the kitchen delivery area. James looked up and said,

'I'm sorry, I'm a bit busy at the moment, could we talk later?'

She sat down and said, 'You're not fucking too busy to talk to me. I'm your superior now, so you can fucking shut up, and listen to what I have to say.'

She could see him give in. He was so weak. Why did he take this crap from her? Why didn't he just throw her out? How could she respect someone like that? Men should be strong if they were going to be attractive. But if they were that strong, they might be able to dominate women. Oh, fuck all that. The fact was they shouldn't be as weak as James.

'Did you get those drawings I sent you all right?'

'Yes, yes, thank you for those. Very interesting. Thank you'

'You need to start excavating then.'

'Archibald wants Cairn-Brown to do most of the excavating work. I'm under a bit of a cloud.'

'Cairn-Brown had an accident on the way to his excavation.'

'God, what happened? Is he going to be all right?'

'Not an actual accident, unfortunately. His pathetic body is as it always was. But I fixed it that the university has approved him going to a week's conference in America right in the middle of the excavation season. He's over the moon. Why are people always so keen on conferences there? It's been a dire experience when I've had to do it. So now you're in line to do an excavation this summer.'

'It'll have to be something to do with Byzantine trade routes.'

'Anything's a potential trade route.'

'It needs to be plausible, and not too big because the budget's been cut.'

'Which gives you?'

'Hindley Grange.'

'Right. So, you're not just a pretty face,' Branwen said.

'It's on a river. There was a wharf at least as far back as the thirteenth century, so there could have been something earlier, and the drawings could point to a religious complex. Unfortunately some of that could have been damaged when they dug the foundations for the nineteenth century house.'

Hindley Grange, she recalled, had been an impressive pile built by a successful nineteenth century brewer. It was burnt to the ground in 1895, after a maid dropped an oil lamp near some curtains. Now only some charred walls hidden amongst brambles remained. The drawings came from an amateur dig in Victorian times, when the brewer had hoped to establish some form of continuity between his own house, a farm that had stood somewhere nearby in the Middle Ages and the Roman villa. Those faded, yellowing drawings, and a few coins in a local museum were all that remained of the heat and sweat of Victorian labourers and the ponderings of bearded country gentlemen in a long forgotten summer.

*　　*　　*

'It isn't working,' Lizzie said.

'What isn't?' James said. She was propped up against pillows in the motor home.

'Us. I mean, don't get me wrong. It's been fun. But it isn't going anywhere.'

'No? Why not?'

'You know why not.'

'No'

'It's her'

'Her?'

'Helen.'

'Helen? I haven't had anything to do with her since last summer. She shafted me. I haven't forgotten that.'

'I'm sure you haven't. I'm sure you haven't forgotten anything about her. That's the problem. No one can have a proper thing with you, while you're still mourning her. As the saying goes, there're three people in this relationship, and it's kind of crowded.'

'What am I supposed to do?'

'Seek closure, or whatever they call it. Talk to her, electronically at any rate.'

'She's probably got someone else by now.'

'And that makes you sad. I can see that.'

'Well . . . I don't know . . .'

'You need to understand what went wrong, accept it and move on. Knowing she was with someone else might help you do that.'

'So you wouldn't be my assistant again?'

As it was only a small excavation, and Lizzie had worked two previous summers on a site, this had been sufficient for her to be James' assistant at Hindley Grange.

'I'm happy enough to work with you. Colleagues, that sort of thing. I'd come down to the pub and have a drink. But, a relationship, no. We're probably not that well suited in any case. You dream, you speculate, you have theories. I think that's something you had in common with Helen. I'm more interested in people and their reactions to what we find in the ground.'

To himself James admitted that much of what she said was true. Their time at Hindley Grange, sharing the mobile home, had been a thing of lust for a pretty girl, mixed with an attempt to stifle the surprising amount of pain coming from the rift with Helen.

Lizzie got out of bed and started putting her clothes back on,

'While we're talking of Helen, perhaps I should send her a thing on what we've found here, for her holoblog.'

'Hold on a moment. Archibald will hit the roof, if he thinks she's got hold of an uncensored account.'

'Too late to worry about that. I had something from Branwen just before lunch—I was meaning to tell you. Archibald's worked out that you conned him when you chose this site. It's that drawing of the nineteenth century excavation. Apparently his PA managed to find a version of it on some obscure hobbyist site. Even then Archibald was too slow to realise what it meant. It took a bit of brain massage to convince him there were signs of a religious complex. He's already told Branwen that there's definitely no more excavations for you, lad.'

'I see. Well, I'm afraid that could spell journey's end for my time at this university.'

'Have you got something else fixed up?'

'Possibly. Nothing definite though.'

Andrew had offered him that job. But informally, an easy flattering thing to say in conversation. Things like that had a habit of evaporating the moment you tried to call them in. He would keep a low profile until he had a signed contract in his hand. But at bottom, he was through with Archibald's determined lack of intellectual curiosity. He wanted out.

* * *

Ten years ago it had been a revelation to James to find informed people willing to discuss unconventional theories, but as the years passed these meetings had begun to weary him. These faded hotels in obscure London streets. Disorientated tourists in the foyer, and then the long journey down corridors to find the meeting room, and the long fallow periods of speakers who weren't saying anything he hadn't heard before.

The coffee break seemed more promising. He'd force himself to overcome his natural shyness and network with these people. He only really come because Terence Hill was speaking on Celtic religion. It was Hill's book on the fourth century religious thinker, Pelagius, that had sparked off James' interest in post-Roman Britain and its religion. A knot of people had already gathered round Hill. When James came up, Hill was saying something to a woman about the survival of paganism in the post-Roman period.

'I seem to remember your book on Pelagius suggested that his ideas accounted for the post-Roman take over by Christianity,' James put in.

To his surprise and dismay, Hill gave the impression of recoiling at the mention of his own book, and his expression became slightly disdainful.

'Well that was a long time ago, a bit out-of-date now,' Hill said. 'Er . . . I don't fully go along with that view any more. I mean Pelagius, is certainly important figure, yes, very important, but the idea of his influencing Celtic religion is probably . . . er . . . nowadays a bit out-of-date, a bit fanciful, or exaggerated. Erm . . . excuse me, just now, I've got to sort out something about my holo-projector, it's been playing up a bit.'

With this, Hill slipped away from the group around him, and James was left with the hostile stares of the others, who were no doubt rightly blaming him for breaking up their little tete a tete with the luminary. James moved on to pick up a cup of coffee, and then circulate round the room. In doing so, he accidentally found himself just behind Hill, but this time, it was Hill who was the one anxious to gain attention. He was talking to a short grey-haired woman, and James heard him say,

'I hoped you might review my new book. It'll be coming out in time for Christmas.'

'I don't know, I'm really only working part time now. Winding down towards retirement.'

'Crufters are going to publish it this time. I've been working closely with them on the editing,' Hill said.

'Crufters, ah. Well I might see what I can manage then,' the woman replied.

So that was it. A sell out. Crufters would want something with plenty of nice pictures and opinions that reflected the mainstream thinking of thirty years ago. This reviewer was in the same orbit as Crufters, happy to lend her support to the glossy and orthodox. When he had first encountered Hill and some of the others here, they had promoted themselves as being free from the trammels of academic pressure and incentive. But he could see compromise with conformity sapping their energies now. He didn't have much doubt that

Hill had been quietly bullied out of pushing his previously more interesting but controversial ideas about Pelagius.

The mid-afternoon session confirmed James's reservations. Andrea Perkins, another person whose writing on the missions to the Saxons had helped to spark of his original interest in the period gave a not uninteresting talk on the beliefs of the Saxons prior to the arrival of Augustine. But when in the Q&A session a young man asked about the dispute between Augustine and the British bishops, she seemed to James to be following the same route as Hill into compromise with orthodoxy.

'I think Bede is brilliant in how he represents that dispute,' she said. 'He shows it as no more than jockeying for position between Roman and British hierarchies. No evidence of difference in beliefs. The timing of Easter is just a bureaucratic thing. Bede make that brilliantly clear.'

What a cop out James thought. She knew very well that Bede was an apologist for the Saxons and orthodoxy, and that even he had not confined the dispute to the Easter problem. She was taking a safe bet on hardly anybody actually reading Bede. Nobody who read his rather trivial and credulous account would describe him as brilliant. There was a place in this, where she did not want to go.

Her reply was really the last straw. He slipped out before the final lecture could start. The afternoon sunshine beat down as he walked through the park on his way to the hi-speed. He had fooled himself that he could exert an influence on these people. Independent scholars they called themselves. And maybe they once were when they were younger. But they had to scrape some sort of living, and the mesh of publishers, reviewers and lecture circuits had gradually ensnared them in a place where serious subjects were not discussed, and indeed not even regarded as being serious.

From the real blood and iron of post-Roman Britain, they had receded into faery, the realm of Morgan Le Fay and

Excalibur, an enchanted land from which they would never escape. It brought it home to him that if he wanted his ideas to win out, he would have to do it for himself. Unfortunately that meant he would have to give up the secure and respectable for a higher risk route. It was that or accept a smothering orthodoxy for the rest of his life.

*   *   *

This was it James thought. He'd put his signature to the Gate's contract. All that remained was for him to burn his boats here. That made him feel uneasy. Until he spoke to Archibald, he had a relatively secure position jogging on from one month to the next. Afterwards he would be on his own, outside academia, working for disrespected fringe people dependent on the donations of foreign eccentrics.

'You wanted to see me?' Archibald said. 'I can't spare you much time. We've got an emergency meeting coming up.'

'Emergency?'

'Senior expenses committee. One of our wine suppliers has just gone bankrupt.'

'Oh, I'm sorry.'

There was a pause and then Archibald said,

'But you didn't come to talk to me about our wine problem.'

'Er, no. Look, the fact is I've decided to resign.'

'Resign. You can't do that. I mean it's most inconsiderate at a time like this. That idiot Cairn-Brown going off to Germany. He was very scathing about our university and all of us here, I must say, yourself included. And now Trish on maternity leave. You're being very unfair, very disloyal after all this university has done for you.'

It struck James how it was always really callous people like Archibald who were most indignant when someone inconvenienced them.

'I'm sorry if it comes at a rather inconvenient time, and I am sorry to leave, but I feel I have to develop my career, and I've been offered a very interesting opportunity'.

He wasn't going to fall into Cairn-Brown's elementary error of slagging off someone who might still have a future influence on his professional life.

'An opportunity. Where are you going? I hope you're not getting in out of your depth. I've seen that happen before. Young people lured away to a prestigious university, and then finding that they can't cope out on their own. We tend to nurture the, well, yes, the less able person such as yourself here. Other places wouldn't care. They let the devil take the hindmost.'

'I actually thought you'd be quite pleased. I mean we have been slightly at loggerheads over my view of the subject, particularly our post-Roman disagreement.'

'Well, that's what I mean. You don't have the flair of a Cairn-Brown. You haven't grasped the correct interpretation of your period. But here, we can deal with that, we can, in time, develop you into a solid second tier man. I fear for you where you going. Actually, you didn't tell me where it is.'

'I'm joining the Gate.'

James had the satisfaction of seeing real surprise register on Archibald's face

'I didn't realise you were absolutely mad. Look, I'm a decent man. Many wouldn't, but I'll let you retract your resignation. You must realise if you go there, no respectable place will ever give you a job after that. I wouldn't be able to take you back once you've been there, you realise.'

James squirmed inwardly. For once Archibald was saying something sensible. It was an irreversible decision and a life sentence to the fringe. He might almost have considered retracting but for the knowledge that Archibald would hold this over him.

'I have considered that,' James said. 'You're right of course. But I'm not changing my decision.'

'All I can say is that you're a very foolish and, yes, a rather inconsiderate young man.

Archibald's PA loomed in the doorway

'Sir Clarke . . .'

'Yes, yes, I've finished here, I'm coming.

*   *   *

A fly buzzed against a hot window. It was the centre of Nigel's attention. He was scarcely listening to the exchange between the lawyers. Case management conference they called it. Initially an attempt to avoid the expense of a full trial. Sir Trevor, Miss Bell and their lawyer were ranged grimly on the other side of the table. A white haired man at the head of the table was the judge, but wore only an ordinary suit. Next to Nigel, Harold was making some long winded point. Suddenly, Nigel's attention snapped back into place. Something was going on. Miss Bell had asked the judge if their party could confer outside for a few minutes. This request was granted.

When the trio returned only a few minutes later, Sir Trevor and the lawyer still look grim faced, but it struck Nigel that Miss Bell had a rather smug expression. Sir Trevor's lawyer announced that his side had an offer. The museum's displays would be altered to be more in accord with the original agreement that gave more prominence to the idea of the lower church being a baptistery and the possible religious associations of the silver hoard. However, the plaque commemorating Nigel's donation would not be changed or enlarged. Apparently the trustees now considered such a prominent dedication inappropriate.

This time it was Nigel and Harold who were allowed to confer outside.

'It's outrageous, Nigel said. 'Of course, they realise I made the donation for PR reasons. They're just taking the piss.'

'But we should take the offer seriously none the less. Now they've made an offer, if you don't win the whole case, you have to pay the costs of both sides. The agreement on the plaque looks pretty clear, but a judge might think it was all a bit vain glorious, certainly after the amount of trouble that's been associated with the project.'

'I'll risk that. They shouldn't think they can take the piss like this.'

Nigel turned and went back quickly towards the conference room. His was reaching to open the door of the conference room when Harold said,

'Of course if it goes to trial, you could also loose what they've offered with the baptistery and the silver. A judge might take it into his head to consider that it was a reasonable variation of the original agreement.'

Nigel stopped, 'Can we get a coffee, I need to think a bit.'

'Yes, I suppose so, but we shouldn't be more than fifteen minutes. The judge could get impatient.'

They went into a small windowless area that served as a cafeteria and sat with undrinkable coffee at a plastic table littered with dirty plates. Nigel was uncertain. That in itself annoyed him. He was used to knowing where he was going, a pursuing a definite target. Of course, at first sight it was obvious he should reject the offer. The whole point of spending a large sum of money on the museum was to garner favourable PR for his business. Sir Trevor was too stupid, but Miss Bell was a devious and malicious woman. She had concocted this plan with the help of that weasely lawyer of theirs. But Harold's last remark had struck a chord. The actual content of the displays which had been neither here nor there at the beginning of the project had become a factor for him. The image came to him vividly of Helen weeping and Maria trying to console her, when James had cut her off. That had been a consequence of the tortuous arguments over the excavation. Then, although he had pushed it to the back of his mind, there had been that strange experience when they visited the underground church. The sense that this was something important that should not be airbrushed away by meddling bureaucracy. It was infuriating, it went against all reason, and yet sitting there in front of the disgusting coffee, he knew he was going to act on his feelings and accept their offer.

Back in the conference room, he at least had the satisfaction of seeing the other side appear surprised and annoyed by his acceptance.

'Er, we might want to reconsider, could we . . . erm . . . confer again,' Miss Bell said.

'I find this very irregular. You've made an offer and it's been accepted. I can't understand what's changed that you need to confer again,' Nigel said.

'That's right,' Sir Trevor said. 'A man has to stick to his word. Not chop and change.'

Luckily, Nigel thought, Sir Trevor was too stupid to see the problems he might be walking into.

CHAPTER 13

DEATH, SEX AND SACRIFICE

Helen saw her mother lower the big metal platter gingerly onto the polished surface of the table. Another of her father's creations. Gleaming, translucent blue and made from some very costly new composite material, but also incredibly easy to scratch. Anything that had the slightest collision with it would leave its ugly mark and spoil her father's evening.

'It's so seldom we're all three in at this time in the evening,' her mother said. 'I thought we'd have a family dinner. I'm sorry I never learnt to cook properly. There never seems to have been time. But I did organise *Sloane Gourmet* to deliver this. It's a bit extravagant, but you both liked it last time you had it, *Canard à la Sloane*. You needn't look so gloomy, Nigel. Is something wrong?'

'I'm sorry. Thank you for getting this, I've just had some bad news.'

'Oh dear, what's happened?'

'Sir Trevor is trying to back out of our museum deal. And we spent a whole afternoon thrashing it out only a few days ago. The one thing I did credit him with was sticking to his word'

'Oh, no! Why?'

'It seems the ministry is getting back at him by withdrawing the grant to expand his vineyard. You know it's his pride and joy.'

'Can they really do that,' Maria asked.

'Nobody could ever prove what's going on. It's separate sections of the ministry, but for anyone who lives in the real world, it's pretty obviously a fix-up.'

'What are you going to do?'

'I'll instruct Harold to take proceedings first thing tomorrow morning.'

Helen had a sensation of something surging at the back of her neck and then the feeling that her head would burst. Why were they continually blocked at every point in this project? It had all been arranged at the museum, but now they were back to square one again. A court case could drag on for ever with no certain resolution,

'I can't stand this', she said. 'I'm so tired of this museum business. I feel sick. I'm sorry. I don't feel like eating anything at the moment.'

She got up from the table, went to her room, and put on a rubbish film. Afterwards she went to bed but couldn't sleep. She turned the museum problem over and over in her mind. She ought to do something about it. She admired people who had ideas and got things done. That had been the problem with James. He was half way along that road. Half attractive. He had an interesting idea, but lacked the courage to pursue it properly. It was this whole wretched museum business that had broken them up. Regret mingled with anger as she recalled the heat of their summer love making.

But what could she do? Go and see Sir Trevor? He would probably be glad enough to talk to her, but would he take her seriously? He obviously fancied her, but—. Oh, no! How disgusting! How grotesque! She of all people to think of that. She'd often been teased by both males and females about her conservative approach. The last one in her class to lose it, except for Bertha, poor thing. She had always taken it seriously and avoided the casual. James was the only time on a first date and despite everything that had happened that remained somehow special.

Thinking about that made her sad, but also told her what she had to do. Not to be like him, but to take determined action. But it might get out. Or even if it didn't, just the thought of how people would react, if they knew, was awful. How would her parents take it? Would it be anger or shock or a bit of both. Would her father get seriously angry and shout at her? That had only really happened once, the time when the precious Ikea collection got burnt, and then she had completely lost it and broken down in tears. She was grown up now, but it would be just the same if it happened again. As for her mother, she fancied it would be more pain than anger. Even now her mother seemed to be wondering why all the love, thought and money invested in the daughter project had gone strangely awry in bad dreams and frustrated ambitions. And her friends, would they turn away in disgust, while others she knew less well sniggered at her loss of seeming virtue?

But she had to be an adult, a real person, capable of taking control. Not afraid to act like James had been. She had a purpose, and to achieve it, she would have to make a shameful sacrifice. But she didn't really see it as unethical. No one except her would suffer. It was what the Buddhists called harmful but not evil, a bit like smoking, but not as dangerous. Now she felt better, if rather shocked by what she was set upon, and with that she knew nothing until the grey light of morning came in between her curtains.

*　　*　　*

Helen sat in the museum's cafeteria. She felt nervous and a bit sick, and in the cold light of this mundane space she was incongruous. She was wearing her most alluring clubbing and partying outfit, which revealed bits of her or her underwear in unexpected places. Around her people huddled over cups of bad coffee. It wasn't just men who were giving her funny sideways glances in this place.

She had hoped that Sir Trevor would refuse to see her because of the rift with her father, or at least put her off to another day, but no, she had been welcome to come first thing in the morning, or at least what he regarded as first thing in the morning. She considered things a bit more as she sat there. She'd persuade him to have it filmed. It would be set to transmit back to a remote data basis. If he went back on things, she could threaten. Of course if she let it out, the disgrace might be worse for her than him, but she thought she was strong enough for that. She glanced at her watch. It was getting near the time. She felt light headed, almost out of her head, as she walked through the galleries of the museum and then the corridors of the office area. She was aware of Miss Bell, his PA, surveying her curiously, as she showed her through to Sir Trevor's office. She noticed him shut down a screen rather quickly. Probably watching porn.

*　　*　　*

That nice red-haired girl was just taking . . . , but then Sir Trevor had to shut the film off. Helen had arrived a little quicker than he had anticipated.

'Helen, how nice to see you, you looking . . . er . . .' he said, taken aback by her appearance, and then continued. 'I haven't seen you in ages. I'm afraid . . . this disagreement with your father. But you're too young to understand that.'

She surprised him by coming over and sitting on the corner of his desk, so that he got the full benefit of her thigh, and then placing her hand over his. It was exciting, but also concerning. She normally seemed to try to put a distance between them. He worried that she might have been seeing a boy, and getting forward ways before she ought to.

'The argument with daddy is what I've come about. He's very upset and he's going to talk to his lawyer. I thought the two of us could resolve things before there's any nastiness.'

'How sweet of you, dear girl, but you're too young to understand. Even I don't understand it properly. I can't see why your father is so cross, or why those awful little people from the ministry are so cross either. But I've been over it all with my advisers. They say they don't think I'll get the grant for my vineyard, if I put what your father wants in the museum. Dear girl, the vineyard's been my life's work, you know. I only took on the museum as a duty, because they needed leadership.'

'Can't you pay for the vineyard yourself, and tell the ministry where they can put their money?'

'I don't think you should talk like that. I'm sure your parents wouldn't like to hear you. But dear girl no, the fact is I do need their money. When I was young, I was a bit reckless, and I liked to put a bet on the horses. That always seemed a pretty good way of losing money, but then I discovered prize-winning vineyards. It's as much as I can do to finance the existing acreage. I need the ministry's support for the extension.'

'Then I want you to give that up.'

'No, no, I can't think of it.'

'I've come to offer you a bribe to do just that.'

'I didn't realise you were getting an inheritance. Strange your father never mentioned that. But it wouldn't be enough in any case. You seem much too young to have been allowed to have money like that, and young lady, my advice is that you shouldn't throw your money around. You should keep it until you have a young man and want to get a home.'

'I don't have an inheritance. Bribe was the wrong word. It's really a nice little present for you, – a special treat. What's the nicest present you can think of?'

A dark and inarticulate thing rose in his mind, but he pushed it away and said,

'Dear girl, you're not making any sense. What're you talking about.'

She swivelled round on the desk so that her leg hung down and rubbed against his leg in a pleasing but slightly embarrassing way. The other leg swung free to give a view of its elegant line. She leant back slightly on her arms showing her profile to good advantage, and said, 'What you've always wanted. You can fuck me.'

He panicked. He probably wouldn't be able to satisfy her. He'd look foolish and decrepit. He thought how he'd always fancied Maria, then one day at Nigel and Maria's house, he became aware of the adolescent Helen, as she walked in from the garden—even more beautiful than the young Maria had been. Now he felt his heart, which was the cause of some concern, pounding. She was probably a virgin with fantasies about men. Young women were demanding. They expected excitement. Their men should be like young bulls. But at his age, he needed coaxing and time. He looked at Helen, warm and young, and thought she wouldn't have the expectation or patience for that.

'That's not a very nice word you used, coming from a young woman,' he said, really to buy himself time.

'No, I'm sorry, you're right, it wasn't. I should have said that we can make love.'

'Dear girl, you're a bit young to know about these things, but I think I'd better tell you something in confidence. A young woman comes to cook my lunch most Sundays. She comes early, the part of the day when I have the most energy. She knows about older men. She doesn't mind helping them, because she comes from a rough background. But you've had a good home and things. You could find what I need—well, a bit humiliating.'

'Don't worry. It'll bring out the tart in me. I've had varied boy friends. I've got a good idea of the things men like, and even young men can have their droopy moments. You can do what you like with me. I won't be shocked. Whatever little fantasies you have. We can film it — so you can have something to look at afterwards.'

'At your age. I thought you'd still be — . I'm rather shocked at your experience. You're only seventeen, aren't you?'

'No, twenty-five. But if you prefer seventeen, we can pretend. I can come wearing a school uniform and white knickers.'

'No, no, what you've got on now . . .'

He thought about Ana, the girl who came every Sunday. It didn't seem to worry her. But she was not one of his own people. There was no warmth between them. Her efforts were mechanical for the most part. She looked a bit like Helen, but there was a hardness and a coldness about her that was not just about being paid, but about where she came from. A place somewhere east of east, far beyond the reach of laws and health and safety, with broken pavements, burnt out or abandoned trains and dangerous factories owned by gangsters. It suited her well, their arrangement. Crisp bank notes unseen by tax collectors, some of which went home to grateful hands in crumbling blocks of concrete flats.

Helen was so different. Being near her was like being in the sunlight. She seemed so warm, so redolent of openness and loving people and safe gardens. Somehow sex had seldom been like that for him. His mind went back to his teens. A midsummer night's party in a big garden, the dress pulled over her head and her arms reaching out. But after that it had seemed to be all unloving hearts and cool, distant marriages and now quite alone.

'So, just once?'

'I think so, get it out of the system, but a nice memory, and you'll have the film for those long winter evenings.'

'This Sunday at my place?'

'Right.'

It wasn't much of a bargain. To give up hectares of vineyard to have elderly sex just once. He could see the vines march across the hill behind his house, the appreciative nodding in the tasting marquee at the three cathedrals festival and the golden-green of the wine as he lifted the glass to drink. But vineyards took a long time to grow, while Helen was here and now.

There was a sickness out there in the ocean, so they said. Each year the autumn winds blew more strongly, and when they howled around the house and through the hills, he wondered if he'd live to see the spring. His doctor wasn't very optimistic. Nothing terminal as such, but generally not in good shape. He shouldn't drink so much. She said he would live longer if he went into residential care. No alcohol, more reliable medication and less stress whatever that meant.

He'd visited friends in those places. You were locked in and became a drugged zombie. None of this he thought, glancing at Helen, nor the new wine from his vineyard. But the doctor was probably right about longevity. There might not be much time. He was always at funerals nowadays. His peer group and younger than that sometimes. People he had known disappeared into an over elaborate wooden box. Soon there'd be a service where he was the one in the wooden box. Was there really a place where there were no girls or wine or gardens with herbaceous borders, but just darkness or nothing at all? Probably the doctor thought so, although the two of them would never dream of discussing it, even in a private setting. That was probably why she favoured the zombie plan as being one level better than nothingness. But he wasn't sure about that.

That chirpy little woman that did for a vicar nowadays spent most of her time talking to old ladies in the council houses or organising charity things. He didn't like women vicars, and they were nearly all women these days. He could remember when he was a boy, there had been a grey-haired man with certainties for answers. Still this little woman had seemed very bright and confident about the clear and present hope of resurrection when she did the funerals. Then one day, when he had had perhaps a bit too much at a drinks party in the village, he had tentatively tried to broach the subject with her. She had stared at him as if he were a lunatic, and then had quickly gone off to talk to some other women about arranging a tombola stall. He looked at Helen. Really the answer was obvious.

'All right, come this Sunday at about ten. I'll book *Sloane Gourmet* to do us some lunch for after, and we can try some of the new wine from my vineyard. I hope you'll think it's good. My people say it might win the three cathedrals' prize this year.'

'Done, but I want you to book your contractors to make the museum alterations, and to send me the transcripts of the call to the contractors before the weekend, and it's probably a good idea to phone daddy or his lawyer and let them know you've changed your mind. After that I think we have a deal for Sunday.'

She got up, straightened her clothes, smiled at him, and then he felt the gentleness of her parting kiss on his forehead.

* * *

Nigel came in looking unusually cheerful, 'Great news,' he said, 'the museum've started work on changing the villa display. They had promised, but I wasn't sure if it was just a bit of stalling. Looks like we won't have any litigation after all.'

Maria and Helen both expressed relieve at his announcement, but Helen felt her mother looking at her.

147

'Perhaps you helped Sir T. change his mind,' Maria suggested.

'Who, me! He thinks I'm some sort of air head. Anyway I haven't seen him in ages'. But she felt the colour rising in her cheeks, and realised that her mother would notice. She had often been teased about her tendency to blush easily.

'It's just, I thought someone said they'd seen you at the museum last week.'

'Oh, right, yes,' she said, 'I did drop in to see how the villa display was getting on. But I didn't see anything of Sir T., thank God. Probably watching porn in his office.'

'Oh, that's odd. His PA's with me on the 'Save the Walrus' committee. She thought you dropped in to his office on Tuesday morning.'

Oh, er, right, yes, I'd clean forgotten. I did drop in for a few moments,' Helen said blushing even more. 'Well, you said I should when I'm near there. You said he was lonely and all that. But he would never discuss business or anything with me. He seems to think I'm still some sort of child. Actually I was on my way to meet a bloke for lunch.

'Another archaeologist?'

'Er . . . no . . . er . . . something to do with insurance, I think, but we didn't really click.'

'Pity, but it was very sweet of you to think of Sir T.,' her mother said, but her expression and her tone of voice said "guilty as charged".

Helen buried her hot face in a newspaper to indicate that this utterly shaming conversation was over. The worse thing was that that witch of a PA might have drawn the same conclusion as her mother, and if so the taint of rumour would already be spreading far and wide. The only saving grace was that daddy, floating high up on a cloud of alpha male self-congratulation, seemed to have missed the undertow of their conversation.

Actually it hadn't been as bad as she had feared. To start she'd had to do one or two things that were rather blush worthy, but after that the old goat had come more easily than she'd expected. Surprising given that the rest of him seemed to be a complete wreck. That weekly girl must be doing a good job keeping the engine tuned. Probably the only reason the old bugger was still alive at all.

Chapter 14

True Friends and Others

Helen glimpsed Angela with her glossy shopping bags sitting in the food court of the Galleria. That was really strange, she suddenly realised. She hadn't heard from either Angela or Margaret in ages. Normally, they'd have been calling her to join them shopping. Instead she was here on her own and so apparently was Angela,

'Hello, stranger,' Helen greeted her.

'Hello.'

No smiles or other indications of pleasure at seeing her after an unusually long gap. Helen sat down at Angela's table and said, 'I haven't seen you for ages, what have you been up to?'

'Nothing much.'

'We should all get together some time.'

Angela avoided her gaze and mumbled a yes.

'Is there something wrong,' Helen said.

'No, no.'

'It seems like there is.'

Angela shifted her cup and plate around on the table for no particular reason, and eventually said,

'There's talk.'

'Talk? What do you mean?'

'Surely . . . surely, I don't need to spell it out.'

'Yes you do.'

'The thing at the museum. They changed their exhibition round. They're saying that's because you did it with the old boy that runs the place, Sir Twerp or whatever his name is.'

'I suppose it's his bitch of an assistant that's been putting that around. But anyway, when it comes to it, so what. Have you become some sort of guardian of our morals.'

'It's become embarrassing, embarrassing to be involved with you.'

'What nonsense,' Helen said. 'What if I did sleep someone, that'd be my business.'

'Some people might call it prostitution. But maybe I could live with that if it wasn't part of something bigger, something weird. I don't do weird.'

'Weird?'

'That dancing in the nude business. What fools we looked in front of your parents. You completely shamed us. I mean what was that? Witchcraft? Doing drugs is one thing, I can live with that, but witchcraft and funny religion is over the edge. That's got around too.'

'I can't imagined who talked about that. I suppose James . . .'

'No, I think Margaret blabbed something to her new friend.'

'The fact is,' Helen said. 'I wanted people to know the truth about the villa, the excavation.'

'That's another thing. James might be a decent enough guy in himself, but I've looked up his stuff on the holotext. All that rigmarole about some sort of crusade against a way-out religion. His ideas are near to fringe. He's not popular with his peers. It's a whole nexus of weirdness that I don't want to be part of.'

'This is ridiculous. You're exaggerating the whole thing.'

'Did you ever read the gospels?' Angela asked.

'What?'

'Stuff in the Bible.'

'Er . . . there was something in RE. Wasn't it the bit with parables? Anyway what's that got to do with anything?'

'We did do the gospels in Comparative Media,' Angela said. 'And, well, the bits they give you in RE are a censored selection. If you sit and read it through, there's stuff there that's completely weird, off the wall, people going up mountains and talking to people who've been dead for four hundred years.'

'What's this got to do with me?'

'What I'm saying is that amongst all the dross there is a live wire in religion somewhere, and you've gone and touched that live wire, and blown your mind to jelly. I don't want to be near things like that. I want to have a life with normal people.'

'I thought we were friends,' Helen said. 'Maybe I've had one or two difficulties, but you should stand by people. I'd stand by you, I think.'

Angela sighed and said,

'Were we ever really friends?'

'Yes, of course.'

'I don't think so. You just let us tag along because having us as an entourage made you feel superior.'

'Did I ever say anything to suggest . . .'

'No,' Angela replied, 'you didn't need to. Ever heard of effortless superiority. You had it in spades.'

'How?' But Helen was uncomfortably aware that from the very first minute she had felt superior to Angela and Margaret, but she had just never suspected that they had sensed her private thoughts.

'You had the big house in the village where all the smart people lived. We lived on the twentieth century housing estate.'

'That's not my fault.'

'No, not your fault, but part of your aura of superiority. And you went to Martins of course.'

'Well there you're wrong. Your parents must have spent more money moving house to get you into the academy than mine spent on fees.'

'But going to Martins was still, in your face, superior. And what about university. Quads a subject for high flyers rather than the soft option of Comparative Media, and of course you had to get a first.'

'Well, you've done better since,' Helen objected. 'You got a decent job straight after university, you've bought a flat. I'm only just starting to get things together. I've had a hard time with journalism.'

'I got the sort of job, you're too up market to consider,' Angela said. 'Doing insurance in an office slab. Not for you. You had to have a glam-celeb type career. Well, that's higher vices at higher prices.'

'So, why've we been going around together all these years, if you dislike me so much.'

'In a word, you can pull, and I might get one of the less successful contenders.'

'I've never been able to see that. I think it's nonsense. I mean the only time we did seem to be competing for a bloke, you won hands down.'

'So happened he liked blondes with big bums. Turned out he was a complete jerk as well, so effortless superiority took that trick as well.'

'Does Margaret think the same as you?' Helen asked.

For the first time, Angela smiled and seemed to become more relaxed. 'Margaret's found a new friend, so she doesn't need to hang around you any longer.'

'What do you mean, hanging around me? Well anyway, what's he like?'

'He's not a he.'

'What . . . Oh, I never realised. I thought . . .'

'No, I just don't believe you didn't realise all these years,' Angela said. She was hopelessly in love with you from that first day at university. When it was she and I together, most of her conversation was about what was the chance that one day you might get round to shagging her. Once you put your arm round her for some reason, and she dined out on what that implied for the next year.'

'But it's ridiculous. Are you sure? I mean there's nothing wrong with . . . I mean . . . it's just I never felt . . .' But Helen suddenly realised that this revelation explained a whole lot of anomalies in Margaret's behaviour.

'That's it,' Angela said. 'You just didn't really notice us. We were just attendant lords or ladies-in-waiting or whatever. Anyone who was remotely interested in Margaret would have noticed the way she mooned around and gave you bits of soppy flattery the whole time. Anyway she hates you now for disappointing her all these years. The new girl looks a bit like you, but a bit more butch. She must like something squiddgy and passive. Margaret gets tied to the bed post apparently.'

'Sounds fun.'

'Yes, it certainly seems to be that.'

'But that still wasn't a very nice thing to say about your friend, squiddgy and passive, I mean.'

'No, but you think just the same.'

Angela got up, gathered her shopping bags and said, 'Good bye, Helen.'

'Perhaps we'll meet up for coffee sometime.' Helen said.

'I doubt it somehow'

Angela turned and made her way down the concourse of the galleria. Looking after her, Helen thought, yes, it was true that her legs were too short and her bum was too big. Really Angela's attitude was completely ridiculous. What if she was brighter and more interesting to talk to than Angela and certainly Margaret. That wasn't her fault. They should have been grateful to be allowed to hang out with her all these years. The truth was they were boring and she was well rid of them. The only annoying thing was that she had let them be the ones to break off the acquaintance.

*   *   *

Nigel watched the headlights trace the hedge row as he drove the last stretch of country road towards home. He had seldom been so angry. It had been a tedious reception at the town hall. He had been surprised when that poisonous Miss Bell had sidled up to him. Their conversation didn't last very long. She was skilful with innuendo. Without really saying anything very much, she had resolved something that had puzzled him, the reason for Sir Trevor's U-turn over the museum exhibition.

He didn't care that Helen was twenty-five, he would say some things about what she had done that she would never forget. How could she think to behave like that after the way they had brought her up? Was there anything in their life that suggested what she had done was acceptable? Hadn't he set a good example? Going out every day to earn their living. Succeeding because he worked hard. Getting things done . . . Oh no!

The blue light of a recharging bay appeared ahead and he pulled onto it. He leant forward onto the steering wheel, seeing the silhouettes of trees against the night sky. Only the occasional lights of a late commuter disturbed his thoughts. Now he started to see where he had gone wrong. His example had been rather too bluntly that one should win out. That was the message he had given. And of course it was an ugly truth that a woman could use her body for that.

So then it was Sir Trevor who was at fault. He was an old friend of the family. Well, not really a friend, a business acquaintance, but he had been treated like a friend. It was one thing to be a dirty old groper, they could treat that as a bit of a joke, but he should have known better than to accept such an offer. Nigel set off again, this time heading towards Sir Trevor's place. He would confront him. In previous centuries they would have fought a dual. Sir Trevor couldn't have managed swords, it would have had to be pistols. He knew exactly which bit of Sir Trevor he would have aimed his shot at. Nowadays one was supposed to use fists. But that was no good, he might kill the old man. Even a verbal confrontation started to seem risky. He remembered how Sir Trevor didn't look too hot that time he had berated him at the museum. He'd have to just send a message expressing his disgust.

He had joined a larger road, and now the garish lights of a junk food outlet loomed up ahead. "We pay the carbon tax increase for this month", a collection of orange bulbs assured him. He pulled into the parking area and set himself to compose something good. The trouble was that he was at home with figures and with visual patterns and volumes, but the written word didn't do things for him. "Keep your hands off my daughter." seemed a reasonable start, but what he really wanted was some pithy insult. Here he couldn't rise above of a ten year old in the school yard. Eventually he managed, "You disgust me, you senile hyena." Would that do? What was a hyena anyway, some sort of predator in Africa, but what did it look like? After some fiddling, he managed to get the image of a hyena on screen. Ugly brute, but there the resemblance to Sir Trevor ended. The animal was a strong athletic natural borne killer, quite unlike the doughy, sluggish hulk that was Sir Trevor. He needed something else. What about that fish-type thing that Maria was keen on. Yes, that was it, a walrus. Some more fiddling and the image of a walrus appeared. That was more like it. The beast seemed to exude some of the blubbery ineffectiveness of Sir Trevor. One could envisage the Sir Trevors as an endangered species. He could imagine the commentary, "This fascinating species is threatened by the destruction of its habitat, slightly decayed minor country houses surrounded by fine vineyards." But somehow the word walrus wouldn't fit itself into a telling insult. Eventually he had to settle for "Keep your hands off my daughter. You disgust me."

He was about to send it, when he paused. Two things; firstly, Sir Trevor might try to change the museum back, if he realised the thing was public knowledge. There was presumably a tacit threat of disclosure that had been held over him. He might be sufficiently out of touch never to discover that it had become public gossip. Surely, Helen hadn't made a film to threaten him with. He felt certain she wouldn't have gone that far.

The other concern was that there had been the beginning of a rapprochement between himself and Sir Trevor since the end of the museum dispute. Sir Trevor's trust owned the shops on the run-down north side of Brindle Gate. If Nigel's firm could get him to deal, they might be able to upgrade the whole street. He ground his teeth. The fact was that he was just going to have to live with it.

Arriving home, he glanced into the dimly lit living room. Maria and Helen were at opposite ends crouched studiously over the glow of their screens. So seeming innocent. He went to his office and looked round. Saw the row of toby jugs on the recessed shelves. How he hated them. Had to keep them because they were old and had been in the family etcetera. He picked up the nearest one, and hurled it across the room at the valuable but hideous cabinet, also old and in the family. The jug shattered and left a scar on the cabinet. He took another one and another.

'My God, look what you've done. What's happened. Those were nearly two hundred years old, and you've ruined that cabinet. You'll have to clear this up yourself. I'm not going to do it, and it's too embarrassing to ask Mrs. Troughton.'

Maria had come in behind him, no doubt attracted by the crash of china.

'I've always hated them, but I was told I had to keep them. They were in my bedroom when I was a child. They used to spook me out at night. I felt they were looking at me.'

'We could have sold them, what on Earth's come over you.'

'I discovered something very bad today, but I'm not going to talk about it.'

'Ah, I see,' Maria said. 'You've found out at last. I knew straight away, but you're too wrapped up in yourself to be aware of something like that.'

'It's my fault, I suppose.'

'Yes, she's learnt to be a bit ruthless in the pursuit of her ends. She didn't get that from me.'

*   *   *

Helen spotted an unexpected name amongst her messages. Branwen; what could she have to say to her? She opened the message.

'Wow! I thought you were just a bit of juvenile arm candy when I found you with James. How wrong you can be. I've just picked up on how you fixed the museum. Even I would draw the line at that old goat. That does really get respect. If you can do that, you certainly deserve something better than James. — Branwen

She didn't know whether to be pleased or angry with this message, but what predominated was that annoying sadness that any mention of James always brought on.

Chapter 15

Home Truths

The train slowed as it passed between the grim ranks of small Victorian terraces. A place that people came from, but never went back to. It was always the same when he arrived here. James had a sinking feeling, and a slow settling of depression. Emerging into the station forecourt, he viewed the line of bubble taxis. In another town, he would have taken one of these to the inconvenient district that was his destination, but he had left here before the age at which he would have thought of taking a taxi. On the other side of the forecourt he could see the bus stand. The thought of the jerky little bus with its noisy children and grumpy old people was not enticing. He decided to walk. It was welcome exercise after the time in the cross-country train.

He headed along a busy road full of the snarl of vans and the grinding of small lorries. The Victorian terraces gave way to long lines of pebble-dashed semis and bungalows. He seemed to have entered a time warp. He had been away for sixteen years, but in a changing world this was a bubble where things never changed, or if they changed at all, it was only to confirm a slow hopeless decline. Paintwork peeled a bit more than it used to, a newsagent was boarded-up, the last butcher had morphed into a holo-arcade with a bouncer who looked reluctant to let James even pass along the pavement. His parents' bungalow stood on a small crescent lying back from the main road, seeming to attempt, but entirely failing to achieve, a certain exclusivity from the squalor of the main road.

Behind it, on slightly rising ground lay the better area of small detached houses with gardens, where he had started life, before the catalogue of failure and bad luck had brought the family to this lower level. On the forecourt of the bungalow, he spotted the new car. It looked to him much the same as all the previous cars they had owned, or had been forced to sell in financial emergencies, as far back as he could remember. He had quite forgotten this last purchase until now, but realised he would be subjected to a long dissertation on the merits of the vehicle.

His mother and father greeted him. There was the usual momentary high, when he hoped that this one visit would be different. A huge media complex dominated the living room. There was a constant flickering of screens and a background burble of sound as various quiz or game shows progressed. The parents settled into substantial arm chairs that filled much of the rest of the room. James lodged himself on something like an upgraded deck chair that had been his perch since they were downsized to this bungalow more than twenty years ago.

His father did not disappoint. He started to regale James with a long description of various features of the new vehicle parked outside. James would have liked to have relaxed, and let his father get on with it, but he knew that this was the easy bit, and that a more difficult stage was coming. His father switched to interrogating James about the performance of his own wheels. He had helped James with his last purchase, but as someone who seldom spent a night away from home, he failed to see the potential advantages of a mobile home, and could not grasp why James' choice was determined by the interior accommodation. 'Surely, you don't really need a double bed', James was repeatedly advised.

His mother started serving lunch. This was on trays, so they could remain at their stations in front of the media centre. James declined anything on the excuse of a large breakfast. He found their food too heavy and stodgy nowadays. He would have desperately liked a glass or two of wine, but they never drank, and it never seemed to occur to them that visitors might like a drink. Alcohol was a currency reserved for Christmas and birthday presents. His mother frowned, and said that James looked peaky and needed a bit of fattening up. Lizzie had taken the opposite view that he would look better for losing two or three kilos, and had started to monitor his food and drink intake in the time they had spent together at Hindley Grange.

His father became gloomily transfixed by the media shows. It was his mother's turn to entertain James with hard to comprehend conversation, mainly about the doings of neighbours, acquaintances and their children. As the years lengthened out since he had lived here, these people and their relationships to one another had receded into a confused blur. It was too late to ask for clarification. If he did, the question was always greeted with an amazed response, such as "but you know she moved to Swindon". Eventually the conversation took a more sinister turn. She began to dwell on the charms of other peoples' grandchildren. This had become a problem since he had split up with Branwen. Even his parents had shrunk from the idea of Branwen as a mother.

'I never felt Branwen was quite right for you. She could be a little difficult at times,' his mother said.

From someone who had seen Branwen lose the plot on more than one occasion, not to mention that dreadful first Christmas, this seemed a masterstroke of understatement. There was a pause, while someone was awarded a prize on one of the shows. Then his mother resumed. 'Do you have another girl friend now?' He recognised that this was not curiosity about his sex life, but the purely practical consideration that the manufacture of grandchildren necessitated some form of partner.

'Yes.' He amazed himself. Why had he said that? It wasn't true for a start. He hadn't had a girl friend since he broken up with Lizzie after Hindley Grange. Partly, it was telling his mother what she wanted to hear, but really he realised with a shock, it was because he still thought of Helen as his girlfriend. He had been about to suggest to Helen a meeting with the parents when their break up had happened. For reasons that he had never been quite clear about, he had censored out any mention of Lizzie here. Helen would have tried to charm them, where Branwen could only aggravate them. Worse still, the thought that he would never be able to bring Helen here saddened him.

'What's she called?' his mother asked.

'Helen.'

'You must bring her down to meet us.' James thought he could almost see the grandchildren she was envisaging.

'She's very busy at the moment. Perhaps in the autumn.' That bought him some time. Later he could announce that they had broken up.

The grandchildren question out of the way, his mother launched into a long dissertation about the problems at work. This was a mysterious area for James. The economy of the town depended on a number of large companies that did something to do with data. The purpose of these companies, or at least the parts of them located in this town, seemed to be to close down. The life cycle of his parents' jobs progressed through four stages. Firstly there were rumours of pending redundancies, then an outlying department would close down, then some people in their own department were made redundant, and finally they were made redundant. This period of redundancy could last for anything from a few weeks to over a year, after which the whole life cycle would start up all over again.

Sometimes the process would be enlivened by an acquisition by a foreign company. After this almost everyone would be made redundant, but a bit later similar people would be hired to do similar jobs, before the remodelled company settled down to the usual process of trying to close itself down. Occasionally, the stock of local companies was replenished when a new one was set up. The mayor would attend some form of opening ceremony, and announce a new age of prosperity for the town, but within the year this new unit would be starting to try to close down. In fact, these new companies seemed even higher risk than the more established ones. They were prone to have problems with shadowy entities referred to as the group or the parent company, or to have American subsidiaries that experienced major frauds.

His mother's latest company was in the third stage of decline. The work of a department known as 'special case data' had just been out sourced to North Ranjistan, the latest fad as a place to do whatever these companies did more cheaply. His father's company was only in the first stage of rumours and occasional visits from packs of concerned people wearing more expensive clothes and hailing from the mystic place known as head office.

But his mother's career had been overall more successful than his father's. She was supervisor of something, and could complain about the poor quality and lack of motivation of the younger intake, and the shortage of supervisory staff. It wasn't much surprise to her that with these problems, it was simpler to move the business to North Ranjistan. Apparently the Ranjistanians had a work ethic that the younger locals here conspicuously lacked. In contrast, his father had slid down the scale over the years. For a short time when James was about ten, he had been rather proud of being something called an assistant section head, but now he was just a line worker, and in his late fifties with two decades stretching ahead before he could draw any form of pension, he was considered too old for promotion to assistant section head or anything else.

'But things are still going fine at the university, aren't they?' His mother's face brightened as she said this. His job at the university was his parent's consolation prize in life. As a child and a teenager, he suspected that he had been something of a disappointment and a mystery to his parents. All three of them in the family had been over shadowed by the loudly proclaimed successes of the neighbour's child, Henry. He was always in the first team, while James was lucky if he was a reserve for the despised third team. Moreover, at least in the earlier years, Henry was always top in Maths, that dreadful subject, which everyone agreed was a much truer test of intelligence than anything that James was good at.

Time had not been kind to Henry. His slot in life was as a salesman for mobile homes. James had bought his own vehicle from Henry's show room. His father had come with him on that occasion because he could talk the talk. For some reason the town had attracted a large number of sales outlets for mobile homes. They lay along the main roads that crossed the bleak grain prairies that stretched around the town in every direction. These businesses seemed to have difficulty in existing for more than a year without becoming bankrupt, so Henry endured an even more unstable work life than James' parents.

When Henry was not out of work, he seemed condemned to pass his days in the largely silent show rooms of the mobile home sellers. On the Saturday afternoon on which they had gone to buy James' vehicle, there had been lengthy discussions between Henry and James's father, but the show room had not been disturbed by anyone else, except a couple who had mistaken the colourful flags outside for the local tourist information office.

He suspected that his mother had taken a long revenge for having to listen to Henry's triumphs in earlier years, and

Henry's mother would by now be very tired of hearing about James' good job at the university. His mother had however remarked that Henry didn't have that peaky look that James was getting. But James thought that while Henry pulled the Lizzie's of this world when he was twenty-one, they would be less interested in the decidedly non-peaky shape that he had taken on in recent years.

James realised that he had let his mind wander. There was silence except for the interminable babble of the media centre. He looked across at his mother.

'Things are fine at the university, aren't they?' she reminded him of her question.

This was the moment that he had been dreading and the reason for his impromptu mid-term visit. The moment when he would drop a depth charge into the stagnant little pond of their lives. He glanced at the time. Almost late enough to think of leaving, but no, he had to get it over with.

'Erm . . . I've decided to leave the university,' he said.

It was worse than he had feared. His father switched off the media centre. A grade-one crisis. He had not seen the media centre turned off in the afternoon, since the time the car was stolen seventeen years ago. His mother was rushing in with her damage limitation expertise.

'You're moving to another university,' she suggested in a desperate tone.

'No, it's not a university. You could really call it an organisation for specialist excavations.'

That didn't help much. They had airbrushed out the excavation side of his career, the purpose of which they did not understand, and which no doubt smacked of manual labour, the one thing that was inferior to their own efforts at the data companies. They focused on his lecturing activities which seemed rather grand and important.

'But is it a good job,' his father asked.

'It's quite a bit better paid.'

That didn't serve to impress. What they valued in the university had been the apparent absence of the redundancy cycle that dominated their own working lives. When they were both in work, there was enough money for the car, the media centre and the weekly trip to the mega discount store.

In fact, they had been initially suspicious of his university career as not being a proper job. His father had promoted the idea of a job in a local company, where a friend could feed James the right answers for the aptitude test. They only started to be impressed by the university as year followed year with no sign of redundancy, and after one or two acquaintances seemed impressed by his role.

'Are there problems at your university,' his father asked.

'No, but in terms of career development I need to move on.'

They look puzzled. He realised this comment meant very little to them. Apart from the minor fluctuations of being assistant section head or supervisor, their work always seemed to be the same. He resumed,

'Well, there aren't any problems with the university itself. But there are some problems over my ideas about history — the Saxon period.'

They looked more puzzled. It made him sad. In his mind's eye, he saw a plump young woman in a small garden opening his arms as he ran towards her, and a young man smiling from a deck chair. It seemed impossible that these people and their home had once been the centre of his life. Now there was a frustration in him that there was almost no point of contact with them. They would not try and reach out and understand his present concerns.

He had in the past tried to explain in simple terms his thoughts about the Saxon conquest, but for them history was something rigidly fixed in the picture books of their childhood. The idea of a reinterpretation of that was wholly alien. It was impossible for them to imagine that a civilisation could be destroyed in an argument about religion. Religion had shrunk into such a small corner in their lives that they were not even atheists, it simply wasn't significant.

'You shouldn't have allowed yourself to fall out with your managers. That's a very bad mistake. That's why this has happened,' his father said.

'You should expect to be married at your age,' his mother said. 'That would make you stick with a good job. What does Helen think?'

'She thinks it's time I moved on from the university, developed my career.'

It seemed ironic to him that they were trying to appeal to Helen as a probable supporter for their views when she had worked constantly to undermine his attachment to the university.

'Perhaps she's not a very sensible girl after all,' his mother suggested. 'Could be a bit wild. Is she young? Probably, she's too young. You're not young any longer now, you should find somebody steady who wants to settle down. Young girls are not really for you any longer.'

'The thing you say you're moving to. If it's not a university, is it a company of some sort,' his father asked.

'Not really, I think you'd call it a charity or a trust.'

'A charity,' his father said, 'that couldn't employ you for any length of time.'

It had been a mistake to use the word charity. They would probably be thinking of it as a few coins rattling in a box somewhere. James tried to rescue his position by saying,

'They receive very large donations from all round the world, from donors interested in specialised aspects of archaeology.'

His parents frowned at this, and his father said in an authoritative voice that James hadn't heard since he was fourteen 'I find that hard to believe.' In truth James also found it a bit hard to believe, and was worried whether Andrew had not over played the financial prospects of the trust, but he followed up, saying 'The fact is I've decided it's time to move on. I don't want to hang on at the university for another forty years being frustrated the whole time.'

'I'm afraid I see it as your fault that you've lost your job. Lost a very good job', his father said, still with the unaccustomed voice of authority.

'I didn't lose the job, I resigned from it.'

His parents exchanged puzzled glances. That didn't mean much to them either. He realised with a shock that as far back as he could remember, they had never resigned from jobs, the jobs always resigned first.

'Perhaps you can get another university job. They must have jobs for people who've been made redundant.' She seemed to envisage the entire labour market as an endless treadmill with redundancy and recruitment as ends in themselves.

'I'm sticking to the job I've just accepted for the time being, but it's not impossible I might go back to a university one day.'

'The sooner the better,' his father said.

'I think we won't tell anyone round here that you've lost your job,' his mother said, 'they've always been a bit jealous of us having you doing so well. There's no reason why they should find out, and you'll probably get another job soon.'

He despaired of them. He glanced at his watch. 'I'd better be going, I'd like to catch the 6.10.'

'Well don't go yet. I just saw the bus go down the road, there won't be another for twenty minutes. Your father would give you a lift, except he always gets a parking fine if he stops anywhere near the station.'

'It's all right, I'll walk, I need a bit of exercise.'

'Walk! It's a long way. You'll be exhausted. You should be careful. You're not young any longer, you could strain yourself.'

Why did they seem to view thirty-four as the beginning of the decrepitude. Was it because that was about the age that they had given up hope of anything better?

'You heard what happened to Janet's husband,' his mother resumed.

'No.'

'Silly man. His car was in for repair. He tried to walk to the betting shop on the parade. Of course, he tripped over, broke his wrist and he's never worked since.'

It was no use talking about levels of risks. Their lives were full of sage examples that cordoned them off from any even slightly unconventional activity.

He received a rather chilly good bye from his father in the living room. His mother followed him out into the hall, hugged him, and whispered,

'You see, you'll come back to your senses.'

Walking back to the station, he felt uneasy. Ill-informed as they were, they possessed a sort of common sense prudence, lacking in both Helen and Branwen, who would prefer to see him play for higher stakes, with little thought for the cost to him of failure.

CHAPTER 16

SUMMER IN SALZBURG

Helen almost had to push against the air as she walked across the meadows between the town and the university. The temperature moving up well into the forties. The hottest day in history. The mountains above the city barely visible in the heat haze. Before she could make it to the marble and air conditioning of the university buildings, she spotted a bench in the deep shade of a large tree and flopped down on this. Looking back towards the town, she could see a rounded figure approaching slowly. When the figure got closer, she realised it was Andrew. She had thought she would probably run into him here. This conference was his sort of thing. He greeted her and subsided heavily onto the bench. His face was gleaming from the exertion.

'The conference doesn't seem very well attended,' she remarked. 'The hall wasn't much more than half full this morning. Most people usually manage to attend the introductory thing.'

'You don't advance your career much by attending something like this. You notice there are not many younger attendees. Mainly old gits waiting to be put out to pension or fringe people like us. I talked to a young bloke this morning, who said he could lose his job if the wrong people found out he had been at this conference. So much for the idea that there's a level playing field in science.'

There was a silence as they both absorbed the heat of the afternoon and then he said,

'I've been following your holoblog. It's good.'

'Thank you.'

'Your thing on Wayland's Smithy was new to me. And I thought you got just the right balance with Hindley Grange, questioning the party line, without making more than's justified out of the evidence from the dig. What sort of response are you getting? Is there much interest?'

'Reasonable. Perhaps a few thousand a month. The sort of people who would come to a conference like this, I suppose.'

'Could become profitable in time.'

'Oh no, nothing like that. I don't think it would attract any advertisers, and they say the traffic drops enormously if you try to charge anything. My father's financing me. I don't want to say too much, but he has a bit of an axe to grind with the museum. It shaming really. Twenty-six, no proper job and still living at home.'

'You know that James is joining the Gate next month.'

'Yes, I heard.'

'We've got a really big excavation lined up for him. A place further north, towards the Welsh border.'

She felt tears pricking at her eyes and avoided Andrew's glance. Damn, why did it affect her like this. It wasn't as if they had got on that well in the short time that they were together. She contemplated the green of the meadow in front of them for a while and then said,

'Of course, I'm terribly ashamed of what I did to James. I realised after how selfish it was.'

'But in the end it's done him good. Made him break with the university. He could never have developed there. Would have ended thinking he really believed the party line.'

'I suppose so, but that wasn't why I did it. It was just thoughtless. I really didn't realise . . .'

'I hoped it wouldn't be a problem,' Andrew. said.

'Problem? What problem?'

'James working for the Gate.'

'Why should that be a problem?'

'We're stepping up our output of material. Arguing our case where there our disputes, commenting on anything of interest that arises in our field.'

'That's good.'

'We need more input. Your bit on Wayland's Smithy is just the sort of thing we want. If you want to earn some proper money you can be one of our main contributors. You can still keep on some stuff for your father if he wants that.'

'Would I have to deal with James a lot?'

'We should be able to avoid that, if that's really what you want.'

Surely he didn't think . . .

'I should think it's what James would want,' she said eventually.

She stared out at the meadow for a moment. Surreptiously, she wiped away a tear from the corner of her eye, and hoped that Andrew didn't notice.'

'You could start with a review of this conference,' Andrew said.

'There's quite a lot of the bollocks sort of stuff,' she said, 'but there a few good ideas that never get the attention they deserve. I'll write those up.'

They got up and slowly made their way past large ponds covered in water lilies and into the marble coolness of the university buildings. What had she done? She hadn't meant to agree to that. She'd message Andrew tomorrow, and tell him she hadn't been thinking straight in this heat. But already she was laying out in her mind what she was going to write. And what if she ever did run into James. Everybody had exes, and really they were just two people who had worked together on an excavation one summer, and had a fling. It happened all the time. It should be just a fun memory and nothing else.

*   *   *

It was night, but Helen could see trees here and there silhouetted against the sky and the dark bulk of hills across the valley. Safe at least for the time being. She was on a horse she realised, — strange because she had never learnt to ride, she thought, but she didn't seem to be having any problem with the slight motion of her horse. There were others mounted along with her, women, men and a few soldiers. Elsewhere she could hear the sound of loaded carts bumping over the rough, pot-holed road. Some talked in muffled voices of the white town, a place further to the north. She was aware somewhere in her mind that she was in that other country, the country of her flight from the villa and the fire in the night. But this time there was nothing frightening. She was sad because she was leaving her home, but content that they were going somewhere less troubled.

She became aware of the hum of air conditioning and the pressure of slightly twisted bedding around her. The first hint of another very hot day could be seen round the blinds. So she'd been dreaming, but the same feeling remained with her, the feeling of escape from past problems and unhappiness.

CHAPTER 17

THE DEEP PAST

'It's a wonderful opportunity to support something really worthwhile,' Lizzie said. 'A genuinely good regional cause. Just ideal for giving your company, for the image you're wanting for it. Our audience love archaeology, and they have a high proportion of opinion formers. The thinking person's history. We not afraid to explore controversial theories, but at the same time we're feet on the ground scientific. And archaeology comes over marvellously on Holo 'B'. None of the problems people had with first generation holovision. That's all behind us, thank God.'

'I think you know I've not been very lucky with sponsoring archaeology,' Nigel replied.

Nigel was speaking with his rational mind. He had certainly had a bad experience with archaeological sponsorship. In fact, he was sick of the very thought of archaeology. And that boyfriend, or rather thankfully ex-boyfriend of Helen's was involved in this new thing too. Also, he remembered this girl from last year's excavation. Now it would seem she had moved on to pushing ideas for documentaries about hateful archaeology to gullible sponsors like himself.

It was on the tip of his tongue to dismiss her with a curt mention of being busy, but his glance kept drifting back to the elegant line of her thigh as she sat opposite him. He prided himself on shunning affairs, but he liked the company of young women, and the fact was that he could not quite bring himself to get rid of Lizzie.

'Oh, there won't be any problem like that with this,' Lizzie came back brightly, 'I know all about your difficulties at the museum. But we don't have any of those old dinosaurs or all that bureaucratic meddling. That couldn't be further from what we're like. We're a young company. Dynamic. Flat hierarchy. We're geared to forward-looking entrepreneurs like yourself. Our sponsors have always been very pleased with the results. The Gadzeit holo-survey shows an exceptionally high proportion of our sponsors rated with four or five stars — er — mostly five I should say.'

Nigel reflected that this survey gave his own company one star or at best occasionally two.

'This new dig . . . ,' he began.

'Ah, yes, I was going to mention that. We want to fit the two digs together in one film. The one next to your house and this new one up in the Marches. Of course you can feature personally in both parts. You can comment on how important you think projects like these are. How architects of the modern world like youself realise the need to retain the heritage of the past.'

'Well . . .'

'Look, I know, I've got a great idea. I'm going up to the new dig next week. You could join me on the morning Pullman. No commitment of course. Just a nice chance for us both to look over the new site together.

'Well . . . er . . . yes, that's a nice idea . . . okay, I'll put that in my diary.'

'That's settled then. That's fantastic! You won't regret this. Fantastic!'

He saw a smiling Lizzie to the lift. When she'd gone, a part of Nigel felt angry at letting himself be manipulated by a fast-talking little bullshitter, but another part of his mind had a pleasant warm feeling remembering her neat figure and next week's promised outing.

* * *

'James, you should go down.'

'There's one of your funny lead tank things down there.'

'You've got to see what it's like down there. Great preservation.'

The comments were from some of his young volunteers grouped around the top of a newly excavated well. With them were Nigel and Lizzie. He had to admit she'd done well to get Nigel to consider another archaeological sponsorship after everything that had happened. But James suspected Nigel was still dubious about putting money up. The group parted to let James through to the edge of the well. He peered down. Nasty. Dark and narrow. The flimsy looking ladder trailed off into darkness. He was a bit claustrophobic and didn't like heights either.

'How deep is it?' he asked

'Oh, hundreds and hundreds of metres,' one of the volunteers said, 'but there's a safety harness here for you, certified by the department of health and safety, in the Republic of — sorry can't quite read that last bit.'

Glancing up from the darkness of the well, he caught the glance of Tanya, the most attractive of his female volunteers. He'd made soundings, but she was spoken for by what seemed to be a very attentive boyfriend. There was a slightly contemptuous expression on her face. No doubt she had picked up on his fear. He looked round at Lizzie and Nigel.

'Perhaps our visitors should take priority,' he said.

'I've been down already,' Lizzie said.

'I wish I could go. It sounds fascinating,' Nigel said, 'but I'm getting over a bad shoulder. My physio advises against anything too strenuous.'

James glanced back at the darkness of the well, and then looking up caught a slight smirk on Tanya's face.

'Right, I'd better check it out,' he said trying to adopt an authoritative voice, while already feeling a cold sweat of fear.

They harnessed him up, shoved on a helmet fitted with a head torch, and he clambered onto the ladder.

'Don't worry, I'll dive in to rescue you if you hit trouble,' Tanya said.

As he descended, he heard their chatter and laughter recede. He began to feel totally isolated. Glancing up he could see only a grey circle of light at the end of a lengthening tunnel. His sense of panic increased. He thought of clambering back up, but he could imagine the thinly veiled contempt on Tanya's face if he was seen to chicken out. He should have used Nigel's bad shoulder ploy. But Nigel was a bit over fifty. Over fifty you could use the bad shoulder ploy, and get some sympathy with it, but at his age it would be exposed for what it was. He began to feel a bit suicidal. He had an urge to cast himself off the ladder. But the safety harness, if it worked, would jerk him back from the void, and he would be hauled back up in even greater humiliation than if he had simply backed out. He clung on with now sweaty hands. And it was cold. Getting colder all the time. They could at least have had the decency to offer him a jumper.

But as he went deeper something happened to push his fear further back in his mind. Something that in all his years in archaeology he had not experienced before. He couldn't quite fix his mind on what it was. He supposed it was the direct contact with the deep past. He had lived with carefully labelled plans on computer screens, professionally cut trenches and discovered artefacts neatly positioned on site office tables or in museum displays. Now, hanging on the ladder, he was face-to-face with the cut stone of the Roman well, just as it had been set in place two millennia before. The real unedited, unlabelled past. It was a sense of presence, almost a haunting. He began to dimly understand Helen's distressing sense of a connection to the violent end of the villa next to her home.

At last, he reached the bottom. He shivered in the icy cold, but it was a relief, if only a temporary one, to be on solid ground again, and to have the lights switch on automatically, rather than just relying on his puny head torch. And now he was glad after all that he had ventured down. His team were right. One of those enigmatic round lead water tanks lay right next to him. The outside had the archetypal design for one of these things. The strange idea of putting omega before alpha, the end before the beginning.

But what had those distant people been thinking of when they must have thrown this thing into the well all those centuries ago. If there had been no more use for it, the metal could have been re-used. That signified some symbolic meaning. Either of something bad that had to be consigned to oblivion, or of something sacred that had to be hidden from those who desecrate. And where better to hide it than in water. Because water and springs and wells had a certain sacredness. In myth, the maidens of the wells were supposed to have assisted travellers until the bringers of the new religion had violated them. Fanciful nonsense, but it didn't seem quite so fanciful down here with this mysterious ritual relic.

He started the long climb back up the ladder, eventually emerging dazed into the shock of normality and day light.

'God, you're as white as sheet,' Tanya said. 'Have you seen a ghost down there?'

He was beginning to feel glad she had another male to keep her cheerful. She could probably be a bit of a pain at close quarters. He ignored her comment, and went straight to Lizzie and Nigel.

'It felt like something weird down there, like you were actually in the past,' James said. 'I begin to understand what Helen . . .' He tailed off as Nigel began to frown. He realised that Nigel did not want to have his daughter's strange obsession discussed in front of the others.

'But, it was interesting,' James continued. 'The lead tank being shoved down there ties in with the heresy hypothesis, the suppression of a religion.'

'That's great, that makes a great theme for a film. Just what we want! Fantastic!' Lizzie said.

There was a silence between them after her outburst. James felt Nigel staring at him. He realised that Nigel realised the similarity between his weird experience down the well, and Helen's own disturbing experiences. It was strange, the three of them, himself, Helen and her father, so often at odds with one another, but all bound together by something that bordered on the supernatural.

'All right,' Nigel said. 'I think I've seen enough. You've got something interesting here. I think your film could be worth backing. Lizzie you can get your people to start working on a contract with my lawyers.'

Lizzie looked surprised. James guessed it must have been pretty hard graft for her up to this point.

'This is going to work out great! Fantastic! Really fantastic!' she exclaimed.

That was one thing you could say for Nigel, James thought. He was completely onside as far as the interpretation of the excavation evidence was concerned, and had been sharp enough to spot the opposite view for the official bullshit that it was.

Chapter 18

Edited Out

Branwen viewed their film material with distaste. They called it editing, but really they were asking her to put together an educated type of documentary out of a scrapbook of decidedly variable quality. She'd helped out with this sort of thing before, on the strength of her expertise as an historian, and her known ability to ruthlessly prune the superfluous and highlight the relevant. But she'd never been left so alone on a project. Some of them had buggered off on some glamorous jaunt to Peru, while most of the rest were off for the bank holiday. She'd received the final and totally dishonest advice that there was only an hour or two's work for her to do there.

The fact was that they had left her right up against the deadline, and she was going to be stuck in this place through a long night and possibly well into the next morning. The only staff remaining were a series of willowy clones that answered any enquiry with the same whiny sentence "I don't know, I'm sorry, I've never worked on that project".

She wished she didn't feel she had to take this sort of work. But her position at the university was beginning to look more than a bit shaky. Complaints about her attitude towards some of the students. Well it was true what she had said. A lot of them would be better off working in a the local fish canning factory, helping out whenever the robot canner had one of its funny turns. Of course, it wasn't really the students who were stirring things up, it was the arch-prig itself, Archibald.

Perhaps she shouldn't have told him that his take on Byzantine trade routes was a generation out-of-date. She supposed it was a bit disappointing for him, given that he certainly didn't know anything useful about the rest of history. But what was the point of not speaking out. Wasn't there supposed to be intellectual debate. Well, perhaps not.

She scanned through more of their scrappy, muddled workings. Lizzie's influence here. Her job was conning sponsors into backing their work. All right, she probably had a good line of chatter to bring in the more obnoxious type of sponsor, particularly the male ones. But why did they let her get involved with the actual material. Because she'd talked herself into it, on the back of her supposed archaeological experience, and this explained some of the confused outcome. Now she was off and away, leaving Branwen to clear up her mess.

How'd Lizzie landed that job anyway, after only short spells as an excavation assistant? Well, that was no secret. She traded on her looks. She'd only become even a site assistant in the first place because James wanted to shag her. As for him, he was totally sliding down the slope into the male version of a slut. Helen, public school tart that she was had at least shown some element of substance, but Lizzie was just 'fuck-me I'm fit' and not too much else. It amazed Branwen how she had once been attracted to James because of what she had supposed to be his intellect or ability to formulate and pursue concepts. Well, she had been young then. She had learnt a lot since those times, but James she thought had learnt very little.

Branwen scanned through more of her task. For one thing there was much too much of it. There always was, but this was really to ridiculous excess. Nearly two-thirds of it would need to be cut. Still that shouldn't be too hard. A lot of it was genuinely bad. Had they been pissed when they shot some of it?

And, oh no, this was even worse, that was Helen's father, the pompous idiot. God, she didn't believe he could be spouting this tosh. This was actually embarrassing. He'd thank her for cutting it out. "Modern architects and developers such as myself appreciate the importance of their heritage . . ." Puke! Puke! All he'd ever done had been to make shed loads of money by tearing down heritage architecture. Admittedly it hadn't looked like much to her, mainly betting shops and massage parlours. This read like some sort of mea culpa, public self-humilation. In the long run, he'd be grateful if his crap was cut out.

But wait. He was probably one of the sponsors, and would have contracted to get a given of footage in the finished holo-film. She called up the list of sponsors. No he wasn't there. Strange. Why would they include all that self-promotional guff if there wasn't money in it? What about checking with the others? Oh, it was a Bank Holiday they'd all be off with their nasty partners or their snotty little children. They'd never reply to messages. She did consult a passing clone, but got the usual "not its project" answer.

Okay, then she'd cut that prat of a father right out of it. No, not right out. She'd keep him in the anonymous role of local twat. She kept a shot of him staring rather gormlessly towards that curious piece of surviving masonry that looked a bit like an old tooth in the middle of the site; meanwhile the voice over intoned about a source of fascination to the local inhabitants down the ages.

For good measure she cut out all the footage of James, except for one shot where he appeared to be distracted by the contours of a young female volunteer. But she did decide to let James' batty ideas on a Saxon crusade or whatever it was supposed to be come through in the final version. That would really fuck off the archaeological establishment and especially that prick, Archibald.

*   *   *

James knew he was on the excavation site, but it was strangely different from the usual bleak wind swept pastures. So summery and pleasant; he walked between neat white houses and small but flourishing market gardens. There was bustle. People seemingly moving towards somewhere central. Then without really realising how he had got there, he was in a larger space, an irregular area of cobbles. There was a commotion, and then the arrival of a motley collection of people, some on horseback, some in carts, and others on foot. These straggled to a halt in the middle of the cobbled space. Then he saw her, jumping down from one of the horses. Tall, dark haired and all too familiar.

He woke with a start. For a moment, she sight of Helen was real in the waking world, before he realised he had seen her in a context that didn't exist. Would he never get over what had really only been a fleeting affair. Nothing to compare to the eight traumatic years spent with Branwen, and yet he seldom thought of Branwen nowadays, and certainly never dreamt about her. He thought of Helen lots, but she had disappointed him, and that could still make him angry. Memories of Branwen ought to make him angry, but in retrospect those years they had spent together now appeared more as black farce. He'd mistakenly thought Helen was better, and was angry when he discovered that ethically she was actually worse.

It was getting light and he went through into the kitchen area of the motor home to make coffee. Peering out at the excavation site, he half expected to see the sunny white houses and fertile gardens and Helen springing down from a horse; but there was only the usual bleak wind swept plain and that ungainly outcrop of stonework, so strangely surviving the oblivion of the city that had once surrounded it.

*   *   *

James settled back with a glass of wine to watch the programme. 'The Archaeological Frontier — in new holovision'. He had watched some of the series before, and to be fair it could rise above the general rut of padded out documentary work. As this instalment progressed, his initial fears about misconceptions and misrepresentations largely subsided, and he had to admit that on the whole he was pleased with it. Without taking an all-out controversial position, it had given full coverage to the indications of religious differences between the city uncovered here and the encroaching Saxon world, and it didn't hesitate to link that to the political and military developments in the period.

He was a bit peeved that he hardly appeared in the film, and then only in a slightly embarrassing shot where he appeared to mainly interested in Tanya. Considering the amount of his time he'd spent in front of the cameras, and the care and thought that had gone into what he said, it was surprising that none of this had made it through into the final version. Still it didn't matter that much in his scheme of things. He recognised that he didn't have the charisma or glib talking needed to be a public spokesman. He had to influence thinking from behind the scenes, and in that respect he'd been as successful as could be reasonably expected.

At the same time, he was vaguely surprised to have seen so little of Helen's father. In fact, there only seemed to have been one glimpse of him, and even that didn't identify him, but instead made him look like a casual and not particularly intelligent member of the public. He'd thought that her father was the sole or at least one of the main sponsors of this programme. Perhaps the deal had fallen through, or perhaps the PR people were recommending some kind of slow-burn approach, where Nigel's involvement in archaeology would gradually become more apparent in a series of films.

The programme over, James settled to continue writing up his report on the excavation. Thoughts of Nigel's mysterious non-appearance drifted from his mind. He was determined not to let his first report for the Gate get overdue. He was just putting together a table detailing the date distribution of coins discovered on the site when a bleeper, accompanied by an unnecessary and intrusive shower of muli-coloured lights, announced an incoming holophone call.

Answering, he was surprised to see the clear image of Helen's father projected into the living area. With his new employers, James had none of the old problems with his holophone connection. They used the same excellent Hanki Huukus so smugly recommended by Helen, as used by her father's company.

'Well, at least you're there and answering, and purportedly a human being,' Nigel said.

'Er, yes—have you just been watching the programme. I thought it was quite good actually. Gave a much fairer picture than I was really expecting. What comes out of a holo programme on archaeology is a complete lucky dip normally.'

'Good, you approve. I suppose it was you who was behind this travesty.'

'Travesty? Sorry. I don't understand. You didn't like it? I see the bit with you . . . That was a bit short. You better contact the film makers. I mean . . . if you're not happy' James said.

'A bit short . . . is that what you call it. You think I might not be happy. Look, my time's expensive and I had to spend hours backwards and forwards in front of their idiotic cameras. And that's not to mention the sponsorship they've had. I can't get hold of anyone there, although I'll probably wring their necks when I do. They're going to compensate me for that, and you would too, if you weren't too pathetically poor to be worth suing.'

The image wobbled. Unusual for a Hanki, which probably meant Nigel had disturbed its projection by making a threatening move towards the image at his end. Now the image righted itself.

'Look, I had nothing to do with deciding the contents,' James said. 'It was all down to the film makers. Actually, I spent a lot of time in front of their cameras myself, and that wasn't used either.'

'Oh, I liked the bit where you were obviously sizing up that girl. That's the one thing they got nicely. They've got your number, James, you're good as a womaniser and nothing else.'

'It's really the more surprising my material was cut out,' James said. 'I had a lot of relevant comment on the site. I'd really honed it to perfection with their people.'

'Implying that anything I said would be irrelevant,' Nigel said

'No, no, I didn't mean that at all.'

'The fact is you're behind this. You and Lizzie. You got round her to do this didn't you. I know you've been having a thing with her.'

'Lizzie? Look that was last year.'

'Oh, I see you have a new one each year. Leaving a trail of broken hearts behind you. I suppose the one you were leering at in the film is the latest.'

'No.'

'Ah, well, perhaps she had the sense to tell you where to go.'

'Er . . . Um. Look about Lizzie. It wouldn't have been intentional. She can be a bit scatter brained. You came onto the project late, and she probably simply forgot to add you to the list. And of course, there's the bank holiday.'

'Fuck bank holidays. I haven't taken a whole bank holiday off from work since I started my business. I get sick of hearing bank holidays used as an excuse for every type of inefficiency. Anyway, I'm not buying this Lizzie bank holiday story.

It's your sort of rotten trick to try and stick the blame on a youngster, who isn't here to answer back. The fact is that you have a score to settle with me or my family at least, and you worked it somehow that I got cut out.'

'What score?'

'You were annoyed by Helen's holoblog. You can't deny it.'

'Well, yes. I had good reason. But no. I have absolutely nothing to do with you not appearing in this film. I never saw what you contributed, and they certainly didn't ask my opinion about it.'

There were a few moments of silence. Nigel glanced to the side as if he might be about to disconnect. Then he was lowering at James again.

'Even if what you say is true, the fact remains that you're miserable, small minded and vindictive.

'Well, I don't know — why?'

'Why? Did you say why? Because of the miserable way you treated my daughter.'

'I'm afraid it's more a case of the way she treated me. She effectively destroyed my career.'

'You seem to be doing all right — for an archaeologist, I mean.'

'I'm out of the university mould. Higher risk, less regarded.'

'Maybe, but it still shows you as petty and small minded. I mean we've all cut corners at times. She made a mistake, but there's such a thing as forgiving. She doesn't confide in us, but I saw how upset she was, and I don't get the feeling she's properly over it yet. And you're still pursuing a vendetta against her.'

'Vendetta? What do you mean? I'm not pursuing any vendetta.'

'No? She's got the job writing up, publicising, whatever, for your organisation, and yet you won't let her visit its most important site.'

'No, that's rubbish. All right I asked her assistant to come instead, but I thought it would be awkward for her, and she could always have asked me if she really wanted to come here.

'Meaning you're too much of a coward to face someone you've hurt.'

'Well, I wouldn't . . .'

'Well, you wouldn't, you wouldn't what, you small-minded vindictive person?

The image dissolved is a haze of flashing lights, suggesting Nigel had struck or thrown something at James' holo-image at the other end, and then the connection was gone altogether.

James took a few moments to collect his thoughts after this. But actually the bottom line was not as dramatic as all that. What it amounted to was that Helen was annoyed that she hadn't been specifically invited to the site. And in truth she was in the right so far as that went. Really, there was nothing unusual about exes meeting on a professional basis. He could meet Branwen or Lizzie without anybody getting stressed or upset by it, so why should Helen be any different. Thinking this, he immediately sent Helen a message suggesting she was overdue for a visit to the site.

* * *

The next day James kept glancing at his messages to see if there was a reply from Helen, while telling himself that it wasn't important. The second day he looked less often, and started telling himself to forget the whole thing. Why should she rush to reply. Her assistant had visited more than once, and Helen had posted on the progress of the excavation stage by stage. Anyway, perhaps she was sulking because of not getting an invitation sooner. That was rather what her father had suggested.

The last volunteers had just left for the day, and James was walking along the edge of the site next to the grey tarmac of the lane, which still followed the line of the Roman road that had once passed the city forum. When he saw the bubble taxi turning into the car park, he was certain that it was Helen. He half ran to the car park entrance, anxious unless she decided the site was closed, and went back to her taxi.

Emerging into the parking area, he came face-to-face with her. More attractive even than he remembered. He didn't seem to know how to greet her. Shaking hands was ridiculous in the circumstances, but even a kiss on the cheek seemed dangerously carnal. She seemed to share his awkwardness. They greeted each other with weak smiles, while their arms remained limply at their sides. James led her across to the main part of the excavation. There was an uncomfortable silence for a bit, and then she said,

'Well, how our things?'

'Oh, all right. Certainly, it's easier dealing with this lot than the university and all the crap from the ministry.'

She smiled and said,

'And how are other things? Are you with anyone?'

'Er, . . . No, there was . . .'

'Lizzie, yes, I heard about that. A lovely girl. I should have thought you two would be well suited.'

'It didn't work out. I don't want to . . .'

'No, no, I didn't mean to pry.'

There was another awkward pause, and then James managed to say,

'And you . . .'

'No, there's not been anything . . . nothing important.'

He deviated slightly to avoid a large tussock of grass and in doing this accidentally brushed against her arm. They both drew apart sharply and kept looking straight ahead. Arriving at the main area of excavation, he led her down the steps into a baptistery similar in design to the one she had helped to discover at the Northcombe villa.

'Big,' she said. 'It must be more than twice the size of the one at home.'

'Yes, this was a really important centre in my period. Even more than Northcombe. But there's something up top at ground level that doesn't look much, but is actually more important from an archaeological point of view.'

'To us archaeologists, a post hole can be more important than a portico,' Helen said. 'Well, I count myself as an archaeologist now.'

'This has only been excavated just in the last few weeks. The programme touched on it a bit, but they didn't know enough to quite get the significance. So there's still something new for you to write up. I should have got you up here before really, but . . .'

'Oh, that's all right, I mean I . . .'

James led her to a rectangular area of excavation about fifty metres by a hundred metres.

'Right, this was some sort of stabling and a yard that was used by heavy carts. We've found the ruts made by their wheels over possibly centuries of use. We think they were carrying lead tanks. Well, you know about the lead tanks.'

'Yes, they were always one of your favourite topics when we were back at . . . you know.'

'Yes, I'm sorry, I've probably bored you with them before. Well, they've always been associated with baptismal sites. We've found them in numbers littered around this yard. One was tossed down the well over there. I had to climb a long way down a ladder to get a look at it.'

'You're getting brave.'

'I wouldn't want to do it too often.'

'Trying to impress one the girls.'

'Erm . . . I can tell you, there was something really spooky. Like actually going into the past. I felt I was getting the same sort of vibes you used to get at Northcombe.'

'Good,now you're beginning to get some idea at last.'

'Yes, and it doesn't take a great flight of the imagination to see this as a distribution point for these tanks, presumably taking them out to remoter rural areas for the same sort of rite that they had in the baptistery here. Of course, there's still a mystery as to how exactly they were used.'

'I don't think so,' Helen said.

'Don't think so? Why not'

'Ever tried kneeling down next to one,' Helen said.

'Well, not really, why?'

'In that position someone can duck your head under the water, and hold it there. No need for River Jordan deep and wide. It all happens in your local lead tank.'

'I never thought of it quite like that.'

'Well, I've had time to, working on all this archaeological stuff. You can see I'm not just a pretty face.'

'That's actually a great idea. I'm going to try that argument. Mind you, it's going to be deeply unpopular.'

'You've come home, James. You've come home. Doing the excavations and research you want to do, and not having to hushed up what you find,' she paused and then said. 'Look I know I behaved badly. I'm so sorry, so ashamed. How could I do a thing like that.—I suppose it's a case of good opinion once lost.'

She turned away, but he could see tears coming to her eyes. He was taken by surprise. Somehow the one thing he hadn't expected was weepiness. He'd thought she'd be professionally cool, even a bit disdainful. Her father's comments should have warned him, but he had had a fixed view that she would have moved on, and not be giving much thought to that summer they had spent together. The words "small minded and vindictive" rang in his ears, and he wanted to put his arm round her, but was afraid of being angrily repulsed.

'I suppose I'd better be getting back,' Helen said eventually.

They started walking back across the site. Suddenly he hated the thought of her leaving and the lonely evening that stretched ahead. In the last two days he hadn't really thought beyond the point of when she might arrive. He hadn't considered the question of departure.

'Are you in a hurry, or would you like to come in for a glass of wine?'

He was suddenly embarrassed, realising that this sound remarkably like the invitation that had kicked of their relationship in the first place.

'I'm not in any hurry. A glass of wine would be nice.'

A smile came through now, with possibly a hint of naughtiness, which suggested that the similarity to that earlier invitation had not escaped her.

Once inside the comfortable cocoon of the mobile home, he turned to make for the wine rack, but she yanked him vigorously by the arm and pulled him into the sleeping area, where she started to undo his clothing.

About The Author

Jack Junius was brought up in the English countryside, which forms much of the background of 'The Secret History of England'. He became interested in both writing and the mystical in his teens, but these interests lay dormant for some years, while he was at unniversity and later working in the City of London, which also features in the Secret History. From the 1990s onwards he became interested in subjects such as altered states of consciousness and near death experiences, and the 'Secret History of England touches on these areas.